D0725981

Ron Ellis

Journal of a Coffin Dodger

Published by NIRVANA BOOKS
Typeset by Print Origination (NW) Ltd
Formby, Liverpool L37 8EG
Printed in Taiwan R o C
© 1989 Ron Ellis

ISBN 0 9506201 1 4

CONDITION OF SALE

RON ELLIS

Journal of a Coffin Dodger

Drawings by Sheba Cassini

NIRVANA BOOKS

TUE JAN 1ST

I have decided to leave home. I want to be able to bring the lads back for a drink and a game of cards without upsetting everyone and to play my records until the early hours without getting screamed at for waking the whole house. I would also like to be able to bring a bird back for the night if I want to.

After all, I am 84. It is time I had my independence.

Marge and Neville will not be too pleased. It grieves Marge having me living with them anyway, but she is terrified that I will cut them out of my will if I go. So she grits her teeth and forces herself to pander to my every need.

It was a wise move to allow Marge to believe I have £150,000 hidden away in a safe deposit in Streatham High Street.

Tomorrow I must visit the DHSS to see if they will pay my rent when I find myself a flat.

Marge made cottage pie and Spotted Dick for dinner, forgetting my new vegetarian macrobiotic diet. There was an uneasy silence as I ate my packet of organically grown raisin and cashew nuts, mentioning to them in passing the inherent dangers of eating dead cows.

Once I get settled in my new home I shall start keep-fit classes, get myself into shape, buy a couple of trendy new outfits and see if I can find any nice little things at the Over 60's Night. It should not be too difficult for a man of maturity and culture like myself, and statistics indicate a surplus of widows on the market due to the premature mortality of the English male. My chances appear to be good.

On the other hand, Jim Evans who called round after dinner has not been so lucky. On 37 visits to the Noel Coward Ex-Ironworkers Social Club he has been totally unsuccessful in procuring a woman.

"Where am I going wrong, Walter?" he asked me. "Am I using the wrong denture fixative, do you think?"

"It certainly is a problem, Jim," I admitted. "After all, Tuesday night is Singles Night down there, so if nobody has snapped the buggers up after sixty years of flaunting themselves they must be a pretty grim bunch to start with. And *still* you're not managing to cop off."

Jim looked serious. "I'm beginning to wonder if the wife has been putting in a bad word."

"Jealous, you mean, because she has better luck on the weeks she goes?" I recommended a visit to the Spa Baths at Cheltenham but Jim felt the minerals in the water might aggravate his suspected thrush, so I wished him luck and returned to domestic bliss with Marge and Neville.

1

There was another big row when Marge refused to give Natalie the train fare to Barnsley to man a pit-head picket line.

"But Mum, everyone is going," she wailed.

"Nobody at the Conservative Club is," objected Neville.

"It's monetarist reactionaries like you and Mum who are responsible for the plight of the working classes."

"We *are* the working classes," shouted Neville. "My father was a coffee grinder in Droylesden."

"You can't be working class with video recorders and wall to wall carpeting."

"That is the whole point. We have been elevated into comparative prosperity by the compassionate policies of a caring Prime Minister."

"I thought Mrs Thatcher was still in charge," said Marge. Marge knows nothing about life outside 'Coronation Street' and 'Dallas'. I am surprised she doesn't think she is still voting for Harold Macmillan.

"Assholes," retorted Natalie. You know, I remember little Natalie at five years old, all golden curls, dolled up in a red fireman's jacket, baggy trousers and Wellington boots. She dresses much the same now.

"Thanks to our incredible technological advancement, the working man has exchanged his life of unremitting toil and boredom for a new freedom," explained Neville, who helps behind the bar at the Conservative Club and absorbs their policies along with their tips.

"The dole, you mean?"

God give me strength. The sooner I get to my little love nest the better.

WED JAN 2ND

First thing this morning I was round at the estate agents. I felt rather jaunty at the prospect of flat hunting but this was soon dispelled when old Mr Irving at Irving and Alexanders tried to persuade me to enter warden assisted accommodation.

"There is a bell beside the bed to press in case you need help in the night," he said. I did not tell him that the only help I expected to need would be to bring in the next chorus girl.

My next stop was the library where I picked my way round the unsavoury tramps that regularly haunt the Reading Room and studied the Accommodation To Let column in *The Megaphone*. The most promising seemed to be a place in Stafford Cripps Close, just off the Promenade.

The landlord was a minute, seedy man with a gap between his decaying teeth through which his pink tongue occasionally protruded like a misplaced nipple. He belonged to that ilk of men that one imagines leering through keyholes at partially clothed women.

"You look like my sort of man," he said, as he led me up the stairs. "Here we are, lounge and kitchen with a sea view."

"If you crane your neck," I said. "What about the bedroom?"

He pointed to a corner of the room. "The settee pulls down."

It did not look like it needed much pulling. "How much?"

He deliberated. I managed to gather that it would be £20 a week, or £30 if I was getting the rent paid by the DHSS. I said I hoped to be and he approved warmly. "Most of my people are with them," he said, making it sound like an exclusive club. "They'll look after you, the DHSS. If you stick with them."

I made up my mind. "I'll take it."

"Wonderful. I'm Tommy Murray, by the way. Now just one thing, the bathroom is across the landing. You share with just one person."

I hesitated. "I'm afraid I am not too keen on sharing bathrooms. I was under the impression the flat was self-contained."

"Oh, pity that," said Mr Murray. "The young lady across the way has no objection to sharing with you."

I capitulated. I have always fancied a mixed jacuzzi.

Having secured the flat, I went straight to the DHSS where I was delighted to find that not only would they pay the whole of my £30 a week rent but also I would receive a generous heating allowance to guard my thinning blood against the threat of hypothermia which is rampant in this area. And this in addition to my pension, free bus pass and poor eyesight allowance.

Riches indeed! I am looking forward to being a bachelor playboy again.

Decided to say nothing at home about the flat till I am safely ensconced.

THURS JAN 3RD

I have met the 'young' lady across the landing who shares my bathroom. She is 82 but looks 101. Her name is Miss Newfoundland. She invited me into her lounge for tea and soft biscuits. "It's no fun being 82, Mr Sherlock," she complained, looking out of her bay window across to the distant sea. "I once raced Bugattis along these sands, you know. In the Twenties."

"Really?"

"Oh yes. Men have desired me in their time. I've had lovers in Spain, Italian lovers, Americans in the War; English boys have fought duels over me."

3

"Very cosmopolitan," I muttered chivalrously.

"It's a terrible thing you know, age. I feel no different now than I did then. I feel I could run down these stairs, jump into a sports car and race off across the sands, but look at me." She undulated her skeletal frame. "No man would touch me now, no matter how much I offered him."

"Oh, come now."

"Would *you* care to ravish me, Mr Sherlock, if I were to offer you £100?"

"Well yes, I would *care* to," I stammered, eyeing the bulbous purple veins bursting through the surgical stockings. "Regrettably, however, since the late Mrs Sherlock was taken from me, I have become totally impotent. I *am* 93, you know."

Felt depressed after this encounter so decided not to stay at the flat tonight. Went back to Marge and Neville's in time for dinner. Still did not break the news to them that I am resident elsewhere. The atmosphere was strained. Marge had spent another £30 at Marks & Spencers so she and Neville were not speaking. Apparently it all went on tights and natural yoghourt. Marge spreads the yoghourt on her face to reclaim some of the vast acres of flesh submerged beneath her wrinkles. I presume the tights are for Neville to put over his head to prevent him from witnessing such a spectacle.

I have decided to make love to no more women over the age of 35.

FRI JAN 4TH

Broke the news of my departure to Marge and Neville. Their reaction could not have been any more startling if the Pope had revealed himself on News At Ten to be an Aids victim. Marge rolled her eyes like a black Al Jolson and raved hysterically at Neville. "Now see what you've done. Your Dad's leaving us. I told you not to keep playing those Dolly Parton records, rousing his libido like that. You've made him restless."

"But dearest," stuttered Neville. He always was spineless, even as a young boy. I remember him running home from school at thirteen saying one of the other pupils had set on him, filled his shoes with water, removed his short trousers and rubbed Brasso on his personal regions. They got the girl that did it—a bank manager's daughter called Hilary Hughes. Neville refused to go back to the school unless they put him in a different class, so they put him down a year. Made no difference though in the long run. He was still regularly beaten up but this time by younger and smaller children.

I explained to Marge that Dolly Parton was not, in fact, my reason for leaving. "I want the chance to lead a wilder social life."

4

"At eighty bloody four!" exploded Marge. "And who's going to wash your long woollen underwear?"

I must admit that the domestic arrangements had not crossed my mind. I just assumed that things would carry on as before. Luckily, a propitious reference to the safe deposit box in Streatham High Street saved the situation.

Nonetheless, the hectic events of the week have had an adverse effect on my health. I am suffering from chronic constipation. I have not been since Monday. Last year!

SAT JAN 5TH

Still troubled by constipation despite the bowl of prunes I had for breakfast. No wonder my weight is up from 8 stone to 9 stone 2. 17 pounds of undigested food stuffed away in there somewhere.

This morning I visited the new Hair and Scalp Clinic where they are advertising a miracle cure for baldness. As I have been bald since 1935 I felt it would take more than a miracle, but they did offer a free trial visit so I thought I would give it a try.

In no time I was seated on a high chair whilst a man in a white coat probed around my scalp taking samples of scurf with his tweezers. He proceeded to examine these under a microscope, whistling every so often as if in disbelief at what he saw there.

Eventually he stood up, took a complicated chart from the wall and held it up in front of me.

"You see these diagrams of the head, Mr Sherlock? Well these indicate various diseases of the hair and scalp. You can tell they are diseases because they are written in Latin." He laughed at his little witticism then barked out in changed tones: "You are suffering from *that* disease." He pointed to a drawing of a green scalp with pink segments and a lot of tiny writing. "You will be completely bald within three months unless you start our treatment . . ." he looked at his watch, "NOW."

I sat in a cold sweat. Thank God I had caught the early bus. Half an hour later and I might have been past curing.

He held out a form and a pen. "Sign here. This is for 36 visits of our Special Electronic Treatment." Hands trembling, I signed the form.

"Right. We shall start immediately, not a moment to lose. First of all we wash your hair, such as it is, in our Special Formula Solution." This task he delegated to a young girl with chapped hands. The Special Solution was obviously doing her skin no good.

5

"You've got more hair up your nose than on top," she squeaked joyfully. "Shall I squeeze a bit up there? Oooh, and what about your ears? It's like a forest in there."

I ignored her. This sort of disrespect for the old is typical in the modern generation. I'm glad I was a conscientious objector in the Great War. At least I don't have to torture myself with the knowledge that I fought in the trenches so this lot could live.

When the washing was complete, approximately thirty seconds later, another girl stepped forward with a pair of electrodes which she attached to my bare, wet scalp with suction pads.

"Christ, they're going to electrocute me," I thought, jumping out of the chair, but she pushed me back firmly.

"Don't worry. We're just going to stimulate the hair growth by giving you tiny electric shocks. All you will feel is a pleasant tingle."

I did. In fact it was a *most* pleasant tingle. Absentmindedly, I reached out to stroke her arm as she held the pads in place. She snatched it away.

"Now, now, Shiny. Let's have none of that, you naughty old man." Then she turned to her colleague and whispered. "Did you see that? The dirty bleeder tried to grope me. I've a good mind to give him 2,000 volts."

"Excuse me," I interjected quickly. "What qualifications do you have to do this job?" I was becoming a bit concerned. My head was itching after the Special Formula Solution, and now visions of the electric chair flickered into my thoughts.

"What's he talking about, qualifications?" They both laughed.

"The man in the white coat. I take it he is a trained dermatologist?"

"Cecil? A dermatologist? You're joking. Where'd you get that idea? He used to run a greasy spoon caff on the industrial estate till half the factories closed down."

"Yeah, he opened this place on one of them government grants."

"But all this Special Formula Solution . . ."

She leant down and whispered. "Fairy Liquid. Now lean back else we'll give you a double dose."

I shot to my feet. "I've changed my mind. I'm going to buy a new cap instead."

What a narrow escape! In future I shall stick to Bay Rum.

SUN JAN 6TH

Sunday night and the Over 60's Night at the Holy Mother of Mary in Moses Street. I wore my wide pinstripe suit which is now back in fashion fifty years after Edward G Robinson first popularised it in a Warner Brothers' gangster movie. Round about the time, in fact, that I bought it. The darn didn't show but I inked it in to make doubly sure.

Jim Evans was there, it being his week. He and his wife attend on alternate weeks, never together. Nobody has ever seen Jim and his wife together. It is rumoured that they possess only one set of upper dentures between them so they have to take turns to wear them. They do have very similar smiles.

Jim had again had little success at the Singles Club last Thursday.

"That's 38 wasted weeks now," I mused. "Perhaps you'd better find a different hobby. You spend a lot of time in your outside lavatory don't you? Maybe Origami might be the thing."

It made it no better for Jim to know that Mrs Evans had spectacular successes on her weeks there. Eager witnesses would regale him with tales of her knee tremblers in various shop doorways on alternate Tuesdays with members of the Compton Road Veteran Bowls Team.

There were very few women in the Over 60's that I would have considered entertaining in a shop doorway. Or anywhere else. Lumpy and pear-shaped, they huddled in corners with their Crimplene dresses and bad breath, discussing their operations in anatomical detail.

Billy Reilly was down later. He was telling Jim and I about his recent hernia. It appears the surgery has not alleviated his problem and he is forced to wear a white truss of exceptional elasticity to keep his rupture in place. I had the misfortune to occupy the stall next to him in the Gents after the bingo and he insisted on showing me his scar. It quite put me off my pork scratchings.

By eleven it was all over. What a waste of 20p. Next week I might go to the Grab-a-Granny Night at the Locarno. I believe they get a much better class of geriatric crumpet there.

Back to my new flat for my first night there. And all alone! When I got in, I found that the gas fire is activated by a 50p meter. It must have run out some time before, as ice crystals were forming on the window.

I had no 50p's.

Marge was not pleased to see me at ten to twelve. "A man of your age prowling the streets at this hour. They'll be mistaking you for The Ripper with those nostrils."

She constituted a very ugly sight in her curlers and cement-coloured

7

nightdress which appeared to have been sewn from old parachutes. I explained what had happened but, instead of admitting me to my old room, she disappeared inside, shutting the door in my face, and returning with her handbag from which she extracted two 50p's. "Here. These'll see you through till morning," she snarled, and she was gone.

Does Neville realise what he has married here? No wonder Natalie has turned into a Leftie.

MON JAN 7TH

Day One of my new Fitness Programme. First thing this morning I went down to the Aerobic Academy which has taken over from the old Ethel Wilse School of Dancing. I booked the Introductory course.

It had not occurred to me that I would need a leotard, but the girl in Reception conceded that my combinations would be an acceptable alternative even if they were the wrong colour (off white) and a trifle shaggy round the darns.

I was looking forward to being surrounded by lissom blondes in nylon jump suits but, to my disappointment, we were segregated into two gyms and I had to lie on the floor alongside very muscular youths with oiled skins and small satin pouches containing their personal regions.

We started with press-ups. The lady Instructress, a fierce creature with the walk of a prison wardress, asked for ten but I had to give up after the second because I had a stitch.

I did better in touching my toes (exercise two), but the sleeve of my combinations inadvertently caught on my big toe nail, rolling me up in a ball and requiring four of the oiled youths to disentangle me.

They put me on an exercise bicycle but my feet did not reach the pedals. "We can't adjust it any more," said the Instructress. "Everyone else can reach them."

"I used to be six foot tall," I apologised. "You go smaller as you get older."

"You must be 110 then," sneered one of the youths.

"Why don't you try something gentler?" suggested the Wardress. "Our jacuzzi room is behind the pine doors."

This was more like it. There was nobody else in the pool and the attendant was definitely more on the lissom blonde style so my hopes rose.

"Shall I take these off?" I indicated my combinations.

"Yes, but not in front of me. There is a changing room over there and a towel in the corner."

8

It was noticeable under the bright changing room light how white my flesh was in contrast to the dull grey of my underwear. Maybe I needed a few hours on the sun beds. But first, the jacuzzi.

I slid into the circular pool with jets of water gushing at me from all sides. It felt quite sensual. Carefully, I lowered myself on a raised platform and sat directly over one of the jets. A tingling and not unpleasant sensation developed about my lower person. I relaxed as the water surged up my body. The significance of this escaped me until suddenly I was hit by a terrible pain and fullness in my stomach and a desperate need for a toilet. Clutching myself in agony, I ran to the changing rooms, leaving the towel behind and giving apoplexy to a middle-aged Jewish matron who was emerging from the ladies quarters.

"Are you all right in there?" shouted the attendant after I had been away twenty minutes.

"It seems to be never-ending," I gasped under the door.

"You stupid old man, you've given yourself an enema. Didn't you notice it was a bit painful?"

"On the contrary. It was quite exhilarating for the first few seconds."

It was another hour before I was able to make an ignominious departure. But at least the problem of my constipation has been solved.

TUES JAN 8TH

Spent the afternoon at the Sunshine Club where Old Mrs Pemberton was celebrating her birthday. She generously admits to 97 which I think is a gross underestimate. So many organs have been removed from her in her lifetime that, were one to believe in a life hereafter, most of her is there already, presumably waiting for the rest to catch up.

The Ladies Committee had baked a huge cake, necessary to accommodate the vast array of candles, carefully shaped into a letter M.

"I thought her name was Isobel," I whispered to Mrs Hargreaves who organised the event.

"It is but we couldn't fit all the candles on and so we had to do an M. M for Mrs, you see. Mrs Pemberton. Besides, she's got cataracts. She won't notice."

Not only that but, when she came to cut the cake, the searing heat from the candles was so intense that Old Mrs Pemberton had to stand a good three feet away to avoid third degree burns.

"Pity there isn't a longer knife," murmured someone as she swayed back and forth like a shadow boxer, trying to avoid the flames.

9

"Should she be doing this at all with her emphysema?" pointed out another old crone, as Mrs Pemberton tottered shakily, fighting to draw breath.

"It would be very ungrateful of her not to blow them out," glared Mrs Hargreaves, "after all the trouble we went to making that cake."

"Hold on, she's going." The ageing bag keeled over, a bony hand reaching out to save herself but succeeding only in grabbing the conflagrative confection and pulling it onto the floor where it quickly ignited the trailing stage curtains.

With commendable presence of mind, Mrs Hargreaves ran into the kitchen and brought out a pitcher of cold water which she threw over the recumbent form of Old Mrs Pemberton.

"You fool," someone shouted. "You should be putting the fire out."

"I'm trying to bring the old beggar round, aren't I?"

"Much good that'll do. She'll be conscious just long enough to experience the unique sensation of being burned alive."

Meanwhile, the curtains swung against the stuffed horsehair armchair that was one of the main props in the Mothers' Union stage version of 'Death On The Nile'. It burned a treat. On the floor, the erstwhile cake blazed with the ferocity of a giant Zip firelighter. I had not had so much fun since the Blitz.

"Do something, Mr Sherlock," screamed an old biddy.

"Not me. I'm 84. My doctor says I mustn't have any excitement."

It was a disappointment when the fire engine arrived. The partygoers by this time were shivering on the fire escape, posing for a photographer from *The Megaphone*.

All the chasing about was too much for me. I had to go back to the flat and lie down with a glass of Horlicks. So much for yesterday's fitness programme.

WED JAN 9TH

A quiet night at the Conservative Club Whist Drive. Or rather, it should have been a quiet night, there being nobody there under the age of 65, but things turned nasty shortly before the interval.

I was playing with Mrs Kershaw whose late husband used to be an idle loafer at the Gasworks. She accused me of trumping her trick.

"That was *my* ace," she boomed. "You've just trumped it."

"I'm sorry," I stammered, "I must have made a mistake."

"Too late to take it back," snapped our opponent on my right, a lady with cherries on her hat and loose folds of skin hanging under her chin.

"That's all very well being sorry but I'm 82 for the half with two hands to go. You need new glasses."

"There's nothing wrong with my glasses. Mr Attlee's government issued me with these just after the last War, when glass was glass." I held them out for her to examine but she waved them away.

"Then you must be feeble-minded, that's all I can say."

"There is no need to speak to Mr Sherlock like that." Our other opponent joined in. "It's only a game, after all." This was Mrs Hylands, a school dinner lady who had become a widow some ten years back when her husband succumbed to the wave of East Anglian Syphilis which was sweeping the country at the time.

"It might be a game, but if you don't play to win there's no point in coming, that's what I say. Anyway, he *is* feeble-minded so don't you contradict me."

"I'm not contradicting you. Of course he's feeble-minded. I just said there's no need to tell everybody."

"Everybody knows. He's been coming here for years."

"All the more reason not to waste your breath then."

"Excuse me," I broke in. "If I can explain. You see I thought spades were trumps so I threw away a diamond." By now the bell for the next hand had gone and some of the other players were gathering around our table regarding us with interest, perhaps anticipating a quick round of all-in wrestling.

"Diamonds are trumps," bellowed the awesome Mrs Kershaw, now revealed as a gorgon in paste earrings.

"I know that now," I said sadly.

"And I've got the last two of them which makes eleven for us I think." Mrs Hylands spread the two red cards triumphantly on the baize cloth.

"Two to us," hissed my partner. "A frigging two."

"Really! This is the Conservative Club." The cherry lady clicked her lower dentures disapprovingly and rose to move to the next table.

Mrs Hylands got to her feet. "Are you all right, Mr Sherlock?" She glared at Mrs Kershaw. "He *is* 84, you know."

"So am I," she shouted. "But we could both have been 86 if he'd played his cards properly."

"No trouble is there?" A stooped, gangling figure appeared behind us, hands clasped behind his back and a beatific expression on his face.

"All sorted out, Vicar," said Mrs Rylands.

"That's all we need," seethed Mrs Kershaw. "God's Shop Steward."

"I'll be at the next table if you want me," whispered Mrs Hylands. I seized my opportunity.

"Perhaps you'd care to take tea with me tomorrow afternoon, ma'am, in my new flat off the Promenade."

"That's very kind of you, Mr Sherlock. I'd be delighted."

"Can we get on with the game?" shouted Mrs Kershaw. "Kindly shuffle these cards, Mr Sherlock, and conduct your public lovemaking elsewhere."

"I'll see you at the interval," beamed Mrs Hylands, "and you can give me your address then." She winked as she departed.

So this is it, then. Only five days since I moved into the flat and I am in business. I had better get an extra tin of sardines in. Women like something Continental. It reminds them of Mediterranean lovers.

I hope Marge has done my washing. These combinations have felt a bit itchy since the Keep Fit session on Tuesday. I'd leave them off altogether, but until I get the spare burner for the gas fire it would be inviting frostbite in my personal regions at a time when I might need all the fire I can get.

Oh to be 75 again!

FRI JAN 11TH

Ron Alley arrived on my doorstep after breakfast in a state of shock. Ron is 78 and what they call a 'confirmed bachelor'. I call them 'arpees'— short for Raving Poofters.

Ron had had a nasty experience at the Grab-a-Granny Night at the Locarno last night. He was sipping his lime juice by the bar, minding his own business, when he was accosted by Mrs Washington who coerced him into walking her home.

"I was seduced by the promise of warmed up hot-pot and sweet sherry," he groaned. "She's had seven husbands in her time, I should have known what to expect. She'll have developed a taste for it."

"What happened?"

"I fell asleep, Walter, after the eighth sherry. I could feel her shaking me. 'I know what you're after,' I told her, 'but I've been to Karate classes, I'm a match for you'."

"But you don't know any Karate, Ron."

"Oh yes I do. I go every week to the Zion Self-Defence League at the Mission Hall. We pensioners have to protect ourselves these days against mindless thugs with deprived upbringings and sawn-off shotguns. It's no use holding out a white stick and crying out 'don't hit me sonny, I'm blind'.

They'll just belt you across the ears with an iron bar and shout 'now you're deaf as well you old pillock'."

"You don't have a white stick."

"I do now. The Zionists gave it to me. It's got a sword inside."

"So what happened with Mrs Washington?"

"She realised I wasn't having any, but I had to stay awake all night, just to be on the safe side, in case she took advantage of me in my sleep." He looked earnestly at me. "You've nowhere I can lie down for a bit have you, Walter? I daren't go home in case she follows me there."

A wicked idea came to me. "Just wait there a minute, Ron." I ran across the landing and rapped on Mrs Newfoundland's door. "Could you help me?" I begged. "You did say you were looking for a gentleman companion."

She beamed. She wore a yellow boiler suit that had been invented for someone 67 years younger. She must be the only 82 year old in Britain who buys all her clothes at Chelsea Girl.

"He's looking for somewhere to stay for a couple of days," I explained, "but take it easy with him because he's a bit shy."

"Good news, Ron," I said maliciously, returning to my rooms. "The tenant across the landing will put you up for a couple of days. She's a nervous old soul. Give you the chance to get over things, eh?"

"I'm very grateful to you, Walter. If there is anything I can ever do for you?"

"Give me Mrs Washington's phone number."

No sense in letting good opportunities go to waste. I'll be round there after the weekend.

SAT JAN 12TH

Ron Alley and Mrs Newfoundland are engaged! Mrs Newfoundland popped in after breakfast to tell me the news.

"*He* doesn't know it yet but I've decided to take him in. He is just the companion I've been looking for and so malleable. But pretend you don't know until he tells you himself."

"You will be informing him then?" I said. "But what if he doesn't agree to it? He's never been married in his life."

"I know. Think of it; my first virgin at 82." I shuddered. "He'll be putty in my hands."

The thought was horrific.

Talking to Mrs Newfoundland made me late for my appointment at the doctor's. As usual, the waiting room was crowded with wheezing, spluttering flu victims, spreading their unhealthy germs everywhere. If you want to catch anything, the doctor's is the best place to go.

The only magazines to read were the March 1981 edition of Taxation and a well-thumbed copy of Mechanical Engineering. I was tempted to bring a copy of Lovebirds next time and leave it lying casually on the table. That should raise a few blood pressures during the long wait.

"I want a check-up," I told the doctor when I finally got to see him.

He brought out his stethoscope with a sigh. "It's only two weeks since you had one, Mr Sherlock."

"You can't be too careful at my age. I am 84, you know."

"So you and your medical card constantly remind me. Well, you will never play football again, that's for sure."

"I never played before."

He took out his blood pressure tester and rolled up my sleeve. "And I would not recommend running for taxis." He pumped furiously until the bladder filled.

"I can't afford taxis. I have to run *all the way*."

He checked the bulb and grunted. "Still high. You must come to terms with the fact that there are things you can no longer do. Like you say, you are 84. How long is it since you had an erection, for instance?"

I looked at my watch. "About three hours."

"Good Lord. It's eight years since I had one."

"Well you want to take it easier, Doctor. How old are you? 50? A dangerous age. There is a lot of stress in your job."

He gritted his teeth. "So kind of you to advise me, Mr Sherlock. Do you recommend any particular treatment to alleviate my problem?"

I looked him in the eye. "You might try starch."

That's the trouble with these white doctors. Too absorbed with their own petty problems to listen to the patient. How I got stuck with Dr Gavin I'll never know. Scottish as well. Everyone knows they're not like us. All the people I know have the usual Indian or Paki bloke. Trust me to get saddled with the only whitey this side of Delhi.

THURS JAN 10TH

To Marge's first thing to divest myself of my undergarments which, having been with me since last Thursday, were past their best for exposure to the public gaze.

Marge did not seem ecstatic to see me. "You needn't think you can come crawling back. Neville's let your room to a West Indian brush salesman."

"Just what I needed," I remarked jocularly, "a West Indian brush," but it fell on stony ground. Marge handed me my clean clothes.

"You can change in the bathroom this time but in future you can go to the Launderette. I can smell those others from here."

Had she found out the truth about the Streatham High Street safe deposit?

On the way home, I passed Gilbert's Hair Centre, a run-down ladies' hairdressers owned by an elderly Jewish car dealer who had made a fortune in the War selling black market pork. In his window, amongst the fading cardboard adverts for Marcel waves and the Eton Crop, were a row of white polystyrene heads bearing men's wigs. One of these looked suspiciously like my own hair, last seen 55 years ago. I went in.

"Can I help you?" A black teenager looked up from blue-rinsing the tight curls of a silent pensioner.

"Er, may I speak to a male assistant?"

Gilbert himself emerged from behind the partition. "It's about the wigs," I whispered. Three more ladies, hidden under dryers alongside Blue Rinse, stirred and turned to get a better look at me. "In the window."

"Ah, the wigs," boomed Gilbert. "A nice line, eh? Job lot, only £6 each. How many do you want?"

"Just the one. That brown one in the corner with the Marlon Brando quiff." I kept my voice low. "Is there anywhere I could try it on? In private?."

"We can go in the cellar," said Gilbert loudly, "so long as you don't try it on with me, eh?" He chortled merrily, beaming at the ladies who all laughed back.

I followed him down the stone steps into the darkness. "Isn't there a light?" I asked.

"There will be when I strike a match, hang on a jiffy." He produced a Swan Vesta and tried to light it with the one hand and the box between his teeth. This did not work too well so he brought his left hand into action, the one that was holding the wig, to steady the box. I was able to grab the wig just as the match took a hold.

"Oh, what a lovely fit," he exclaimed, as I pulled the brown hair over my scalp.

"Is there no mirror?"

"Mirror? In a cellar? Hang on." From his top pocket, he produced a pair of cutting scissors which he held sideways up to my eyes. "See?" The match went out and he made no move to light another. "A perfect fit."

"Is it human hair?"

"Is it human hair?" he repeated. I felt he had been watching too many David Kossof films. "For six pounds and he asks if it's human hair." He threw up his hands theatrically. "Of *course* it's human hair. You think Gilbert would sell a synthetic wig?"

"Well . . ."

"Tell you what. I like to help pensioners. Give me a bluey and it's yours."

I peered at him through the gloom. "Done. Er, could you wrap it for me?"

"My life, five pounds and he wants ribbons and bows." But he took it from me as we rose to the shop and crushed it into a waxed paper bag marked Sunblest White Sliced.

I carried it home in great excitement. Purists might quibble that the colour contrasts somewhat alarmingly with the snow white strands of my own hair, not to mention my eyebrows and sideboards, but I don't care.

I put on my brown demob suit to match my new hair and a yellow and green spotted tie I picked up for 5p last week at Oxfam. Resplendent thus, I waited for Mrs Hylands.

Still no sign of her at 3 o'clock. I opened a tin of sardines, arranging them artistically on the two plates. Realised I had no bread but no matter, we could eat them on their own.

At 3.30 Mr Murray, the landlord, knocked at the door. "There's been a lady round for you this morning, Mr Sherlock. Said to tell you she can't see you this afternoon. She forgot she had to go to the Hospital with her feet."

What a waste of my clean underwear!

SUN JAN 13TH

Sunday dinner at Marge and Neville's. Marge had thoughtfully concocted a little nut rissole in deference to my diet. It could have perhaps done with another nut but it was a kind thought. I could not understand her change of attitude until I overheard Neville whisper the word 'Streatham'. Say no more. It looks like I am saved the horrors of the Launderette.

Natalie was missing. She had gone to Greenham Common for the weekend with a party from the militant feminist group, Action Women (no relation to those plastic toys found in supermarkets). They are on joint duty there with Mobile Women whose gaudy bus ambles round the poorer streets filled with demented placard-bearing females, wailing children and social workers carrying obligatory copies of The Guardian.

"What women like these need is a bleddy good hiding," I said to Neville as we discussed his daughter. "Keep them in their place. I'm surprised you put up with it though you always were a weedy little runt."

16

"I think today's woman feels the need to fulfil herself," explained Neville.

"Bollocks. Women are good for two things, that's a biological fact. Cooking and . . ."

"Do you mind," broke in Marge. "Anyway, men are only good for one thing, and that is Providing."

"What about fathering children?"

"We don't need them anymore. There are test tubes for that now."

"You won't get much pleasure from a test tube," smirked Neville.

"You don't get much pleasure from men," retorted Marge. "At least, not the ones I've been with."

"Ones!" exploded Neville. "Ones!"

She could have a point there. Perhaps it was that Brasso rubbed on him all those years ago.

"Anyway," screamed Marge, "you're lucky I haven't gone off with our Natalie and left you to cook your own dinner. Now do you want any more of this Spotted Dick or not?" Neville shook his head and Marge picked up the dish and swept out to the kitchen.

Neville shook his head sadly. "I blame the change of life," he said.

"I had that once," I said. "Must be over thirty years ago, now."

Thank God this feminism has not spread to the Over 70's. At least women of that age know what they are there for, even if they are barely capable of providing it.

MON JAN 14TH

Mrs Hylands called this morning, totally unexpectedly, so I was unable to greet her in my new wig. In fact, I was not at my best at all. My Noel Coward dressing gown had already seen better days when I acquired it at the Seventh Day Adventist Jumble Sale in 1943. Also, I was in the act of cutting my toe nails when she arrived, and the little dish containing the assorted corns, nails and hard skin was still on the table next to the chocolate digestives.

"Cup of tea?" I offered.

"Don't mind if I do." She settled herself on a bentwood chair. When I returned with the two steaming mugs, I found her reading a copy of Fiesta.

"The last tenant left them," I apologised. "I daren't put them out in case the binmen see them."

"I can understand that," said Mrs Hylands, picking up another copy. "They might mistake you for a pervert reading filth like this."

17

"Precisely." I handed her a mug. Little white globules of sour milk were floating on top of the tea, another indication that the fridge in the flat is slightly warmer than the cooker. I stirred it quickly so's she wouldn't notice.

"Just put it on the table," she instructed, "next to those droppings."

"Ah, yes." Delicately, I picked up the little dish and carried it across to the window sill. Unfortunately, my hands are none too steady in the early morning and one of the corns dropped into her tea, but amongst the other white specks it swirled unnoticed.

"I'm sorry to disturb you at this hour, Mr Sherlock, although it is eleven o'clock." She glanced pointedly at the bedclothes lying across the open settee in the corner.

"I can't get it up," I explained, "with my bad back."

"I was referring to the bed-settee," she said haughtily.

"And so was I, Madam. Like I say, it is supposed to fold up but . . ." I indicated the pain in my lumbar regions.

"Perhaps you should see an osteopath. Can I help myself to a biscuit?"

"By all means." I pushed across the packet and watched as she struggled to extricate one.

"They seem to be stuck."

They *were* stuck. I realised what had happened. Last night, I left the stove on by mistake. In the resultant fierce heat in the kitchen, the chocolate biscuits must have welded together into something resembling a Henry Moore statue.

"It doesn't matter, the tea will do nicely." I felt we had not made the best of starts. I made a note to cancel my subscription to Fiesta and replace it with copies of People's Friend and the Catholic Herald.

But the morning was not wasted. After prolonged conversation about the iniquitous rate increases, the rising price of cat food, poor bus services and compulsory euthanasia for politicians over 75, she agreed to come with me to the cinema tomorrow afternoon.

I must make it clear to her that, due to my severe hyperopia, we sit on the back row.

TUES JAN 15TH

A disastrous afternoon at the pictures with Mrs Hylands. I wore my wig for the first time although it was a tight fit under my balaclava helmet.

Severe blizzards and sub-zero temperatures caused by a depression from the North Sea meant I had to wear several layers of winter clothing, making my personal regions inaccessible to wandering hands.

In the event, I need not have worried as Mrs Hylands' hands were clasped in an attitude of prayer for most of the afternoon.

We sat on the back row as I had planned, but I missed most of the first feature as I was trying to remove my balaclava helmet without disturbing the wig. At one point it looked as if they were coming off together, but I managed to seize the Marlon Brando quiff with my teeth as I struggled with the loose strands of steel-grey wool.

This epic battle went unnoticed by Mrs Hylands. Being a martyr to myopia, she was having to use opera glasses to see the screen, concentrating very hard on one of those interminable films about wild geese trying to avoid Peter Scott's prying camera in West Bromwich.

At last, both the balaclava and my ex-army greatcoat were safely deposited on the empty seat beside me and the wig seemed to be roughly mid-centre on my head. The lights went up for the interval.

"That's a curious cap you are wearing," commented Mrs Hylands. "Did you knit it yourself? Mohair isn't it?"

Speechless, I excused myself and, on the pretext of fetching ice creams, I made a quick visit to the Gents to realign the wig. This was not easy with two pimply teenagers looking at me curiously as I swivelled it about under the pretext of combing the Marlon Brando quiff. By the time I had finished, all the Orange Lollies had gone and Mrs Hylands had to settle for a Strawberry Surprise.

The main film had not been on more than three minutes when I realised that something was not quite right. Two naked women appeared on the screen and started embracing. A middle-aged man in doctor's uniform joined them and it was noticeable that he wore no trousers.

"Are you sure this is '101 Dalmatians'?" enquired Mrs Hylands, trying to hold her opera glasses steady as she struggled with her Strawberry Surprise.

I glanced at the screen. The doctor had disentangled the girls and was fondling them simultaneously without his stethoscope.

"I think the Dalmatians come on later. This is just the beginning bit."

The custodian of the medical profession removed his white jacket to reveal a suntanned torso.

"I saw '101 Dalmatians' in 1967. It was a cartoon film. Are you telling me these are cartoons?"

"Puppets, perhaps?" I suggested hopefully, but Mrs Hylands was not put off.

"You had better go to the paybox and find out what has happened."

Reluctantly, I left my seat and wandered down to the booking office. "Can you tell me what time '101 Dalmatians' is on?" I enquired.

"A week on Monday."

"Ah! What is showing this afternoon then?"

" 'Doctor on the Job'."

"A medical film?"

A smile cracked the cashier's face into a thousand wrinkles like a laminated windscreen hit by a passing stone. "No more than 'Car Mechanics on the Job' was a tribute to the motor industry, dearie. That's on in a fortnight."

I went back to Mrs Hylands to break the news that we were a week early. The action on the screen was becoming pretty torrid.

"I don't mind sitting through it now's we're here," I said.

"I can't let you risk exciting yourself watching this sort of garbage at your age, Mr Sherlock. You want to satisfy your appetites with a rich tea biscuit and a nice cup of tea. Leave all that panting and moaning to younger men." She reached over to pick up my balaclava. "Here. Put your other helmet on and we'll pop across to the Fleur de Lys Tearooms. I could do with something warm inside me."

I said nothing.

Two cups of tea and a toasted teacake later, she boarded a bus for home. Luckily, I had retained my ticket and rushed back to the cinema in time for the last half hour of 'Doctor on the Job', explaining to the usherette on the door that I had been out to buy a paper.

I cannot afford to waste my time on professional celibates like Mrs Hylands. Mrs Washington is my next target. She'll find me an easier conquest than Ron Alley.

WED JAN 16TH

Dramatic screams and shouts from across the landing in the night. I was tempted to investigate but I did not fancy the cold lino of the passage in bare feet, Marge's cat having eaten my slippers the previous Christmas. I consoled myself with the thought that it was probably only Mrs Newfoundland being raped and pillaged by nocturnal intruders and went back to sleep.

At 7 o'clock, a fierce knock on my front door forced me to climb out of the sheets. Ron Alley stood on the threshold in a state of high excitement with the news that Mrs Newfoundland had converted him in the night.

"You're no longer a Roman Catholic then?" I said.

"Not that, Walter." He nudged my arm playfully.

"You don't mean the Jehovah's Witnesses?"

He stood up very straight, an imprudent movement which caused his blue striped pyjamas to slide down his hairless legs. He grabbed them quickly. "Mrs Newfoundland and I are to be married," he announced.

So she had got her way.

"Pardon me for saying so, Ron, but I had always believed you were the other way inclined."

"I don't see what being a Socialist has to do with it. Anyway, Jessie has always had natural Marxist leanings."

"I was not referring to your political persuasions," I persisted. "What I mean is, I always thought you were a bit, er, gay."

"Not only gay, Walter, but tremendously jolly now that Jessie has agreed to accept my hand. Of course, as you know, I have never been over fond of all that what you might call physical business, but Jessie has been a revelation in that department. Do you know what she did last night?"

I remembered the screams. So it had been *Ron* who had been raped and pillaged then. By Mrs Newfoundland. Furthermore, he seemed to have enjoyed the experience.

"Not just now, Ron. I haven't had my rice crispies yet."

He departed, still chortling with merriment at his new status. I went back to bed to recover from the news.

I told Jim Evans about it when we attended our usual Wednesday service at the Lazarus Street Spiritual Hall.

"I suppose this will mean another 50p for a wedding present," grumbled Jim, who makes Jack Benny look generous. "They're bound to have a collection at the Sunshine Club and it's not six months since we had to give a pound for Lizzie Bowers' funeral."

"I wonder if she'll come down to the service today?" I mused.

"Lizzie Bowers? She's been dead since last Summer, I just said."

"It's a Spiritualist Church isn't it? That's who you'd expect to find here—the dead."

Jim Evans scratched his chin. "But I've been coming here 25 years and I've not noticed any stiffs in the congregation."

"Well, you wouldn't *see* them, would you? They'd be ghosts. But you have got a point. In 25 years, we could reasonably expect the odd word from a departed member of the congregation."

"That's it, I'm off," said Jim Evans, jumping to his feet. "I'm not going to be conned a moment longer."

"Don't be daft," I said, pulling him down again. "It doesn't cost anything, we get a free cup of tea and it's somewhere to go on a Wednesday afternoon."

"There's the collection plate."

"When did you ever put more than 2p in? That wouldn't get you much in Frank's Caff."

"Well, I'll stop this time," said Jim. "But it's a bit much not getting one message from any of my old mates or my relatives and, God knows, there's enough of the buggers up there by now."

"Perhaps they just don't want to talk to you," I said. This would not be surprising as he's a miserable old sod at the best of times. "Or perhaps they died owing you money and they're frightened you'll ask for it back."

"Hang on," he said. "There have been some messages. That Mrs Hargreaves is always getting them. Some weeks we're hardly in our pews before the tapping starts and we get that wailing voice," (Jim altered his voice accordingly), " 'there's a message from above' (never from below you'll notice, Walter) 'for someone with the initials M.J.' and up the old crow jumps, 'I think it's for me'."

"She's a busybody that one; gets her oar in everything. She's the sort that gets Tannoyed at football matches or has her name flashed on the cinema screen, 'please contact the box office at once'. You might know she'd be first in the queue for a hot line to the dead. When the first flying saucer lands, it'll ignore the White House and land in Mrs Hargreaves' garden."

"I don't know what they find to say to her," went on Jim Evans. "Christ knows, it must be a boring bloody place up there if all they can find to do is ring Mrs Hargreaves every Wednesday."

Perhaps he does have a point. Next Wednesday I think we ought to go down to the Arts Centre and enrol for afternoon classes—Advanced Flower Arranging or maybe 'O' level Lacemaking. Not only will we improve our minds but we might meet some decent new women as well. Intellectuals even. Roll on next Wednesday.

THURS JAN 17TH

Took a stroll in the park at lunchtime and was impressed by the number of shop girls and secretaries tripping about with their pouting lips and tight little bottoms. Realised what I am missing by not being involved in the mainstream of commercial and business life.

After my beans on toast at the Market Cafe, I went down to the Job Centre to see if they could fix me up with an executive position.

"Are you joking?" said the girl behind the desk. "They don't take executives over 45 nowadays never mind 85."

"Couldn't I be a Chairman somewhere? They're usually quite old."

"Most firms prefer to recruit chairmen from managing director level and, if you don't mind me saying so, MD's don't usually come in here wearing old coats tied up with string."

"I lost my belt in the Market Lavatories," I explained. "My hands were numb with cold; your blood gets thin at 84 . . . ."

"If you didn't have holes in your gloves you'd be warmer."

"They're mittens," I pointed out. "Not gloves."

"What was your last post anyway?"

"I was doorman at the Roxy in King Ethelred Street, opposite the Station."

She screwed her face up questioningly. "Woolworths is opposite the Station."

"That's right. That's where the Roxy used to be. They knocked it down in 1947."

"You mean you haven't worked since 1947?"

"1946. Lingering shell-shock you know."

"Lingered a long time, didn't it? Anyway, we've nothing here. Try the window in the corner. They do part time manual vacancies."

The man at the window was no more helpful.

"How about brushing up leaves in the park?" I suggested.

"They tend to fall in the Autumn nowadays, in case you hadn't noticed." He stared at me closely. "I can put you down for next year if you think you'll still be with us."

"Couldn't I be a park keeper?"

"And do some poor school-leaver out of a career? All our park keepers are doing 'A' levels in Forestry and Horticulture. I tell you what, I'll put your name down for Father Christmas as well."

So much for helping the country with its economic effort. No wonder we've fallen behind Korea and Taiwan. Cast on the scrap heap at 84! A lifetime of experience wasted. I'd offer my services to the Red Cross but they might make me drive one of those big lorries across the Sahara and I've always been afraid of lizards.

FRI JAN 18TH

Mr Murray, the landlord, came up to my flat this afternoon.

"There's a telephone call for you, Mr Sherlock. In *my* rooms. I try not to encourage this sort of thing. How did you get my number?"

"When I came down one day to apologise for breaking the seal on the electricity meter, I memorised your number and circulated it amongst my friends and casual acquaintances. But if you would rather have a phone installed in my flat . . ."

"I'd be obliged if you would not give my number in future."

I tottered down to take the call.

"Is that Mr Sherlock?" whined a female voice. "It's Mrs Snape here from the other side of the paintworks."

"Which side is that?" I enquired philosophically. "I mean, it depends from where you are viewing."

"Oh yes, very funny." Her voice assumed the grave tones of a BBC news reader reporting from Belfast. "I am ringing with disappointing tidings, Mr Sherlock, about your friend and lifelong companion, Perce Shatwell."

"Old Perce? What's he done?"

"Well, he's been with me all afternoon and he's not very well."

"Sorry to hear that, Mrs Snape. How bad is he exactly?"

"Well, he's cold and stiff and hasn't moved for twenty minutes."

"I shouldn't worry. We're all like that every Tuesday morning queueing up for our pensions outside the Post Office."

"But he's a funny blue colour, and when I hold a mirror to his half-open mouth it doesn't mist up. I'm afraid he might have gone, Mr Sherlock." She hesitated. "I regret Mr Shatwell may have died an ignoble death."

"Not died with his boots on, you mean. Well yes, maybe Perce would have preferred to have gone in battle, he *was* always going on about the tank regiment although, as far as I know, he deserted when he was 19 and the only tank he ever saw was the one in the loft where he used to hide from the military police."

"No. He had his boots on all right. It was his trousers that were missing— *are* missing."

"Oh God!"

"And I presume you would prefer he was returned to his good lady wife in pristine shape?"

"You mean with his trousers on? Yes, I think so. In the circumstances." Perce's wife being a prim woman who restricted him to one carnal encounter per lunar month, it did not surprise me that he had sought solace elsewhere. But it made it doubly important that he returned home

24

in a condition that suggested he died over-eating at a Freemasons' Dinner. Which meant reinstating him in his trousers.

"I'm at 65 Cedar Road, behind the . . ."

"Paintworks. You said."

"Not bad news is it?" enquired the landlord, eager for gossip. "I didn't hear you say someone had died did I?"

"Only my uncle's gerbil," I said. "Choked on its own vomit." I counted the change in my mock-leather purse, a Christmas present from Marge in 1967. "Might I ring for a taxi?"

It took up the rest of my pension for the week but I have always been a man of decisive action. And Perce would probably have some loose change he'd have no further use for.

Mrs Snape's house was a small terrace with sooty windows. Chip trays and empty Cola tins covered the soil where the garden should have been.

She greeted me at the door, dressed in a soiled apron over a pair of pink slacks, two sizes too big. I am not keen on pink slacks on women over 70. She had thinning grey hair and a small body devoid of any protuberances that might have aroused a normal man's desires. But obviously she had aroused Perce Shatwell.

"All this is too much for me," she wheezed. "I'm asthmatic, you know."

"Well it was certainly too much for him."

She conducted me to the front upstairs bedroom where the stiffened figure of my onetime dominoes partner was propped up on its shoulders with both legs up against the wall.

"Unusual wallpaper," I commented.

"Do you like it? My late husband chose it. He said the blue and yellow stripes reminded him of the deckchairs at Frinton."

I moved closer to the body. "Er—strange position he's in." Could he have been decorating the ceiling, I wondered. Surely not. Not with his feet.

"Mr Shatwell had just paid his respects to me when he emitted a short gurgle and . . ." her voice trailed off.

"It's funny he didn't fall over."

Her face turned a deep shade of puce. "I was perched on top of Mr Shatwell at the time. I probably held him in place."

"Until rigor mortis set in, you mean?"

"I think I must have dozed off. I often used to doze off while Mr Shatwell was taking his pleasure of me. He didn't like to hurry things. It took him time to get his steam up sometimes, you understand, with him being a retired gentleman."

"Had you been in this position all afternoon?"

"Oh no, only for a couple of hours. The first time . . ."

"The first time?" I interrupted. "You mean he'd already, you'd, er . . ."

"Oh yes, he was a man of stamina was Mr Shatwell. He had already taken his pleasure once before we recommenced proceedings."

"Not a man to rest on his laurels, eh?"

"More on his elbows, I would say. The mark of a true gentleman, a man who rests on his elbows."

"What about you? Did you rest on yours?" She looked blank. "I mean, he wasn't a big man. You might have crushed him to death."

"No dear, not the way we were." She took my arm. "Would you like me to show you?"

I jumped back as she steered me to Perce's cold white arm. "I see what you mean about his wife," I said quickly. "It won't do to take him home like this."

"His wife thinks he's at the British Legion Crocus Exhibition." She sniggered secretively. "Come on then, help me on with his trousers."

"Good job he kept his combinations on," I observed.

"Oh yes. Perce always believed in turning off the damper when you'd got the fire well stoked."

"We'll have a job with him in the taxi like that."

"Unless it has a roof rack."

I scratched my balaclava. "I think it might excite too much attention in the town if we parade him round up there. Besides, how will we explain his unfamiliar position?"

"I was thinking before. If you turn him upside down, you could pretend he'd been playing golf."

"In boots? No. Anyway, he never played golf in his life. He couldn't walk more than ten yards without panting."

She looked at me sharply. "You do surprise me."

"Have you got a black bin bag?"

"That's more like it," she smiled. "We'll probably need two unless . . . no."

"Unless what?"

"I was thinking, if we cut his hands and feet off but we can't do that, his wife would notice they were missing. Besides, I've only got a bread knife."

That was it. "It's no good," I said. "We'll dress him then we'll call an ambulance. We can say you found him collapsed outside your house. They'll straighten him out all right."

She looked doubtful. "If you think so. I tell you what, I'll put a couple of crocus bulbs in his jacket pocket. That'll allay suspicion."

"Where's the phone?" I asked.

"I haven't got one. You'll have to use the paybox on the corner."

Better still. I could phone on the way home then I needn't be around to answer any awkward questions. "I'll just look in his pocket and see if he has a spare 10p," I said. "And a bit for the taxi. Now don't you worry, Mrs Snape. It'll all get sorted in the end."

I made my departure. Poor Perce, but what a way to go. I would like something similar myself. To die astride a 16 year old Italian gymnast whilst celebrating Everton's victory in the FA Cup.

SAT JAN 19TH

Called at Marge and Neville's on my way into town this morning. Their daughter Natalie, my grand-daughter, was there. Since she went to College she has changed beyond recognition. Her once golden locks have changed into purple spikes and she wears a diamond stud in her nose which, in a poor light, looks like a burst blackhead.

"Hi Walter," she greeted me. "Coming into town?" She has started calling me by my Christian name which I feel shows a lamentable lack of respect, but when I mentioned it to her she put the blame on me. She said it was typical of my generation's inability to adapt to changing social structures in a non-nuclear society. Needless to say, she is studying Sociology.

Marge looked disapproving. "She's going demonstrating again."

"In Debenhams, you mean? Cosmetics is it?"

"No. Outside Debenhams. She's turned into a Leftie. She's joined the Miners' Strike."

"But she isn't a miner."

"We are showing solidarity with the miners," explained Gnat as she now spells her name. "We collect for them every Saturday in the town centre. I tell you what, Walter, you could come with us. In that old coat, you look a bit like a starving miner." She indicated my best Crombie, still tied with string in place of my missing belt. "We can dirty your face up with coal dust . . ."

"You will not treat your Grandad like that in this house," broke in Neville with a rare show of spirit. "Coal dust indeed."

"We've got gas central heating anyway," said Marge.

"Don't worry, Walter," said Gnat, as if it had been my idea. "We'll get you some soil from the garden on the way out."

I didn't object. It meant a free lift to town, albeit in Gnat's awful Robin Reliant. We parked in a side street behind the Fire Station. A fair crowd had already milled outside the store, spilling over the kerb and thrusting fat yellow plastic canisters into the unwilling faces of affluent Saturday shoppers, most of whom looked like they would welcome the sight of Arthur Scargill swinging from a gibbet outside the Town Hall. The canisters bore the inscription 'Coal Not Dole'.

"These don't look much like miners," I remarked, looking at the motley collection of State-pampered students. Six of them wore Sony Walkmans and were gyrating to an unheard beat as they circulated among the crowd rattling their boxes. Five black ones had dreadlocks halfway down their backs which would have caused serious problems at the pit face. The girls were dressed in white fur jackets or Pierre Cardin raincoats, neither of which were likely to be seen descending the pithead cage.

"You're our token miner, Walter. Here, throw your cap onto the floor, we don't seem to be doing too well with the boxes."

She tossed my cap on the pavement and straightaway someone threw five pence into it.

"I'm getting wet," I murmured.

"That's the spirit, Walter. Play for their sympathy. Can you cough now and then?" I cleared my throat.

"A bit harder, Grandad," bellowed one of the Rastas. " 'ack a bit."

"I'll get you a placard," said Gnat, "to put over your coat."

Drizzle fell steadily as I stood in the centre of what was now a circle as the crowd became an audience and watched me choking.

"Has he lost his violin?" I heard a lady ask.

"Someone help him," cried a lady with a Tory hat.

"He's a miner. They're collecting for him."

"A miner, eh?" The Tory lady turned round and spat. I was able to duck in time but noticed a globule of phlegm trickling down one of the Sony Walkmans.

"Here we are." Natalie returned with a white card on which she had written in black felt-tip 'Fourty Years Down The Pits'.

"You've spelt forty wrong," I pointed out.

"That's what a good college education does for you," she replied. "We're protesting about the standard of teaching when we've finished with the miners." She peered into my cap. "You're doing well," she approved. "There must be a pound in there already. Think of the joy that will bring to some starving miner's family."

"The peak's gone sodden," I said glumly. "Once they've gone sodden, that's it. You might as well throw the whole cap away."

"You can get another at Oxfam for a few pence. Better condition than that thing, too."

"Your grandmother bought me that hat."

"It's time you had another then. She probably got it from Oxfam herself."

A fifty pence sailed through the air into the cap.

"Thank you lady," shouted Gnat. "Support the miners."

"Hang on," cried a voice. "That's Mr Sherlock from the Whist Drives. He's not a miner."

"He used to be," countered Gnat quickly. "He's retired now, Pneumoconiosis."

"He never did. He used to be on the boiled ham counter at Cope's Sausage Stall on the Market. He was there all between the wars. He's never done a proper man's job in his life. Look at those hands—lilywhite."

"Imposter," someone shouted. The mood was turning ugly. "String him up," yelled another.

"Who the hell is she?" seethed Gnat.

"It's Mrs Jessup. She goes to the Whist Drives."

"Tell her you'll cut her in for half if she keeps her mouth shut."

"She wouldn't do a thing like that. She's a strict Catholic. Her husband keeps graven images on the sideboard."

"Oh, all right then, if she's a Bible thumper—three quarters."

"It's no good, I've been rumbled. We'll have to make a quick getaway. Fetch the car round."

"It's pedestrianised. You'll have to run with us."

"I can't run, I'm 84." I stooped to pick up my drenched cap but there was money in it and one of the dreadlock brigade beat me to it. A large woman grabbed my arm.

"I want my 50p back."

"Help," I cried. Mrs Jessup moved towards me. "I've been abducted, Mrs Jessup. I don't know these people."

"Fetch a policeman. This old man has been abducted," she echoed in a stentorian voice. "Let him breathe," she hissed as people closed in nearer to get a better look. "Can't you see he's been abducted?" I allowed myself to fall into Mrs Jessup's arms. "Help me," I bleated, clinging on tight. "Don't let them miners get me."

"Is he dead?" called someone.

"I think he's fainted."

"My cap," I whined. "They've stolen my cap for their evil doings."

30

"After them," trumpeted a middle-aged huntsman, but of Natalie and her clan nothing could be seen.

"All my pension too. All gone."

"Shame," they chorused.

"Here, let's have a whip-round." A Scottish pound note came fluttering down and I reached out a trembling hand to assist it into my pocket. Coins began to fly from all angles.

"Eighty five next birthday." I managed my first tear of the afternoon. Mrs Jessup collected the money.

"What's the trouble?" A policeman with a large Alsatian burst into our gathering.

"This old man was robbed and beaten up by a gang of teenage hoodlums," ventured an eye-witness, "pretending to be miners."

"Are you all right, sir?"

"No, he's not," said Mrs Jessup sternly. "We must get him to a doctor."

"I'll radio for an ambulance. He might have broken bones. Just wait quietly, sir, we'll soon have you in good hands."

"Pardon?" I looked up from counting the new collection.

"He's 84," said Mrs Jessup.

There was £15.73p.

The policeman peered at my placard.

"They tried to strangle him with their posters," explained someone helpfully. "They were miners."

"We'll get in touch with your family for you," offered the policeman

"They're away in Israel," I lied, "visiting our relations. Just take me to the Hospital, I'll be all right."

"I'll come and see you, Mr Sherlock, don't worry." I hadn't taken much notice before but from my vantage point sitting on the pavement looking up Mrs Jessup's tweed skirt, I was suddenly aware she had not got a bad pair of legs for a woman of nearly 60.

Why have I been wasting my time all these Saturdays? I could have made a fortune on a spec like this not to mention the lady shoppers. As for Jim Evans and his Singles Nights, he'd do far better playing his accordion outside Marks and Spencers.

The ambulance arrived and I was laid on a stretcher. "Can you come with me?" I hoarsely urged Mrs Jessup. "It looks very dark inside."

"I have my shopping to do, Mr Sherlock. But don't worry, you'll be looked after now. I'll call in the Hospital to see you tomorrow."

I reached the hospital just too late for lunch.

SUN JAN 20TH

Have spent a most unpleasant two days in the Otis Redding Memorial Hospital where I am being treated for concussion.

I have not had a moment's rest since I was brought in yesterday lunchtime.

The first thing they did was strip me down to my combinations (which were luckily clean from last Thursday) and sit me in a wheelchair with just a thin white robe around me looking like one of the undead in 'Dracula'. I was placed in a corridor outside the X-Ray Department where the draughts from an outside door had me shivering violently.

"Can't I have a cup of tea?" I beseeched a passing nurse.

She looked at my shaking hands. "Certainly not, in your condition. You're in shock."

"What are you going to do with me?"

"X-Ray your head, of course, but you'll have to wait your turn. It's Saturday afternoon, there's a match on."

Eventually, I was taken into the X-Ray Department where my head was photographed from every conceivable angle. Whereupon I was wheeled into Casualty for another hour's wait whilst the plates were developed.

An assortment of badly bruised youths bled quietly beside me, all staring into space. A boy with a pan on his head was led by his mother down the corridor, muffled screams emitting from near the handle. Twice, stretchers were rushed in with dying patients and all the staff ran out to thump them and administer the kiss of life.

I began to wish I'd not bothered coming.

"Right, Mr Sherlock, doctor will see you now." I was wheeled into a cubicle and the screens were pulled round. The doctor was holding my plates.

"No evidence of brain damage," he smiled cheerfully. He looked all of 19 and ready to shave any day. "Have you lost your sense of taste?"

"The only thing I've lost is my cap," I said.

"Nonetheless, one can't be too careful at 84. I think we'll have you in for observation." He shone a light in my eye, grunted and disappeared.

I was wheeled up to Men's Medical where the Sister greeted me with a scowl and divested me of my combinations, replacing them with hospital issue pyjamas. She handed my combinations to a nurse.

"I think these can be thrown away," she said, holding them at arms length distastefully. "They're full of holes."

"They're my best pair," I protested, "and clean on." But she ignored me.

"Complete rest, small amounts of fluid and plenty of sleep for this one," she instructed.

"Excuse me. I wonder if you've any pyjamas with longer legs?"

She glanced down. "They reach your ankles."

"The left one may but the right one only reaches my knees." I turned round to demonstrate.

"It won't matter under the blankets."

They lay me flat on my back on the bed and pulled the covers so tight round me that I was unable to turn over much less sit up. "Now get some sleep," they ordered, but gnawing pangs of hunger kept me awake.

Twenty minutes later it was teatime. A clatter of plates and pans rolled through the ward like thunder.

"Are you having nothing?" asked the man next to me, a small creature with a royal blue dressing gown and renal calculus.

"I'm on fluids," I said sadly. Sure enough, an hour later, the nurse brought me a small glass of water.

"Can't I have Lucozade?" I whispered.

"If somebody brings you some, you can."

"But nobody knows I'm here."

"In that case, I'll draw the screens round you. It's visiting time shortly and we can't have you interfering with the jollity of the occasion."

Visiting time seemed to last an eternity, the noisy incessant chatter completely drowning out the radio on my headphones as small children clattered noisily on the tile floors, occasionally peering round my screen and shouting 'Eh Mam, there's a corpse in here'.

From time to time, just in case I should doze off against all the odds, a procession of trainee doctors took it in turns to haul me to a sitting position and take my blood pressure.

At 9.30 came The Last Supper. Cold cocoa was distributed by an apologetic night nurse who explained that the beverage had started out as lukewarm cocoa but the kitchens were a long way from the ward.

Finally, at ten o'clock, it was Lights Out.

Peace at last, I thought, but I was mistaken. A slight noise from the next bed caught my attention. I listened carefully. There it was again, a tiny gurgle followed by a trickling sound.

Then, from the other side of the ward, almost like an answering cry, came a popping noise reminiscent of a champagne bottle being uncorked. I waited. The unique explosion of wind being loudly expelled occurred simultaneously in two areas near the windows.

Within seconds, the ward was alive. It was like sleeping on the factory floor at Schweppes. Assailed from all sides by frenetic bubbling, popping,

33

fizzing and trickling, I buzzed urgently for the nurse.

"It's their bags," she informed me. "Most of the men in here have had colostomies. It's a popular operation at the moment. One in eight men end up with bags, and one in five suffer from some bowel disorder once they reach the age of 50."

"I'm 84," I said, "and my equipment works perfectly satisfactorily in every way."

"I'm glad to hear it, Mr Sherlock," she said. "Now perhaps, would you be quiet and let the others get some sleep."

"The only way I'll get any sleep in here is with an anaesthetic. Can you arrange it? Listening to those bags filling up is like having Niagara Falls on your doorstep."

"You'll get used to it," she said.

She was wrong. A sleepless night ensued although it didn't last long as Roll Call commenced at 5 a.m. when the breakfast nurse arrived to wash and drug us.

"Just fruit juice for you, Mr Sherlock."

"I want All Bran," I said, "in order to forestall the plague of bowel trouble affecting one in five of the over 50's."

"Bit late aren't you? You should have thought of that 40 years ago."

"I want to go home."

"Doctor is seeing you this afternoon. Just try to rest."

"Rest? In here? I've known quieter munitions factories."

The doctor showed his face just after lunch which in my case was another glass of concentrated orange juice with additives and colourings. Hospitals are bad places for healthy eaters like myself.

"How are you feeling?" he said, consulting my chart.

"Terrible. I want to go home immediately to give myself a slim chance of recovery."

He pursed his lips. "What exactly did you do?"

"Very little. I dropped my cap in the high street and landed up in here. God knows what'd happen if I did something serious like fall off the edge of the pavement."

"Has nobody been to claim you?"

I looked up. Was I in the Lost Property Department after all? "Nobody's even been to *see* me."

"I'll get the Almoner to trace your next of kin. Meanwhile, continue to rest and we'll see what visiting time brings."

Visiting time brought Mrs Jessup and a pineapple. "Better for you than grapes," she said.

"Yet not as easy to peel, but never mind." I put it on the locker next to the water jug.

"You look very cosy and peaceful, Mr Sherlock. You want to stop in here as long as you can and have a good rest."

No word from Marge and Neville and they should have been told by now. The second night promises to be as bad as the first.

MON JAN 21 ST

Woke looking like a hooded crow after a second night disturbed by the musical bowel disorders of my companions.

The Almoner called to see if anyone had accepted responsibility for me. Apparently they had not succeeded in contacting Marge and Neville. Neighbours said that they were in Nottingham trying to remove Natalie from a picket line where she was ruining the family name.

"Somebody must be able to take you away," she said exasperatedly. "What about your landlady?"

"Hardly know the man and I never see the neighbours. Can't I be put in a home?"

She looked amazed. "You mean you *want* to go into a nursing home?"

"Yes please. One where my every need will be catered for by caring people and custard is served at every meal."

"Why haven't you told your son and daughter in law of your wishes?"

"They're keeping me with them hoping that if I hang on long enough, I can look after them in their dotage. But I've made my first strike for freedom—I've got a flat."

"I must see what I can arrange about a Home for you, you poor man. You shouldn't have to fend for yourself like this."

"Not at 84, no."

"I'll contact the Social Services today. In the meantime, I suppose we'll have to keep you here."

"I'm quite prepared to discharge myself."

She brightened up. "That will please the sister. Er—she is rather short of beds."

"I know. More artificial digestion cases, I believe, pouring in by the minute. An epidemic of them. At least you'll save on bedpans."

I was out by lunchtime. Treated myself to a taxi with my 'takings' from Saturday and enjoyed a Winter Hot Pot with Organic Vegetables at the Nutters Bar Health Food Cafe.

In bed and asleep for three. Peace at last.

TUES JAN 22ND

Contrived a meeting with Mrs Washington at the Red Cross Bring and Buy for Ethiopia Sale where they allow you to swop up your old clothes and rubbish for even older clothes and rubbish in exchange for a small fee.

Mrs Washington was doing the teas. She was a large woman who could have competed in the women's bodybuilding leagues with some success had she been fifty years younger.

I introduced myself as a mutual friend of her one time suitor, Ron Alley. "The less said about him the better," she snorted in a voice that suggested that she classed Ron alongside Goebbels and the Kaiser.

"When I say 'friend'," I backpedalled hastily, "I mean, he lives across the landing from me."

She turned sharply. "He does not. He lives in Lenin Close next to the old slaughterhouse."

I explained he had recently moved but this presented more problems.

"He's not living with another woman is he?"

"Er . . ."

"Well!" She looked livid.

"I've just come out of hospital," I said, conversationally. "I'm 84."

"Did you want some tea?" she asked absently, her mind on her recent spurning.

"Do you serve lunch? I've not eaten since I came out." I explained about the recalcitrant cooker at the flat.

"We don't." She regarded me closely. "But perhaps you'd care to take some supper with me at my place this evening. I live on my own since my last husband passed on."

So Ron Alley was right. The woman was obviously dynamite. And not a day over 69. I accepted the invitation immediately.

Mrs Washington lived a good mile from the flat so I walked slowly to conserve my strength for what might lie ahead.

"I hope you like suet dumplings," she greeted me, "with neck of lamb and black puddings." I decided this was no time to appraise her of my macrobiotic diet. "Take your coat off, Mr Sherlock. Or may I call you Walter?" she added coyly, informing me I would be permitted to address her as Vera.

We ate from trays balanced on our knees, perched on an old settee which bore the uncomfortable indentations of previous occupants. There were cowheels in the lamb casserole.

"I've got some nice sherry trifle and cream for later or would you prefer Spotted Dick?" Before I could answer she had filled a tumbler with a golden liquid and handed it to me. "We might as well finish the port before we start the sherry." I groaned. It was like being back at Marge and Neville's.

The meal over, she opened the sweet sherry and refilled my tumbler. "We won't bother with proper glasses, I hope you like it sweet. My late husband did."

I was becoming sleepy. I blamed the roasting coal fire, the sweet sherry and the tedious conversation. Mrs Washington was describing at great length her life with seven previous husbands, most of whom had expired of exhaustion in late middle age.

As we finished the meal, feeling that something might be expected of me, I slid closer to her on the settee and put a tentative arm round her shoulders. Swiftly, she twisted herself round, forcing my head into the suffocating depths of her ample cleavage.

"Take me, Walter," she cried, her voice wailing with paroxysms of rampant desire, a condition with which I had not been familiar for some 20 years.

I did not comply right away. A curious numbness seemed to have affected my personal regions. I wondered if my combinations were too tight and restricting the blood supply to my vital organs.

"Is anything the matter, Walter?" Her hand reached down to investigate. I tried to jerk away and in the resultant melee my wig caught on the exposed shoulder clip of her longline brassiere, disengaged itself from my head and came to rest affectionately over the swelling slope of her left breast.

"Good God!" Mrs Washington jumped up in horror. "What is it, a rat?"

"I've never seen a lady with a hairy chest before," I mumbled with an attempt at humour to lighten the situation.

She inspected the Marlon Brando quiff and my denuded head before inquiring in Lady Bracknellish tones: "Have you any *more* appendages, Mr Sherlock, that I ought to know about? Perhaps you might care to draw up an itinerary."

I wondered about my teeth. Would they be classed as appendages? I had had them for 17 years and had come to regard them almost as part of me. "Everything else is my own, I assure you."

She glanced down in the direction of my personal regions. "Pity. A piece of mechanical apparatus might have been useful in certain quarters." I wilted further under her scornful glance. "I don't know what's the matter with men nowadays."

"Never happened to me before ma'am. Perhaps the sherry . . ."

"Would it help if I removed my clothes? Is the sight of a naked body likely to resurrect your desire?"

"Mine doesn't. I see it in the mirror every morning."

She was down to her woollen vest which reached her knees.

"Gosh, is that the time? My bus goes at ten. I'll have to be off."

"Wait." She struggled with the obstinate garment. I turned away my eyes and searched for my greatcoat.

"No, it's the last one. Thank you for the supper." I made the front door inches from her grasp. In her exposed state, she was unable to follow me into the street.

Ron Alley did the right thing. What happened to the days when Man was the Hunter?

WED JAN 23RD

Met old Albert Gouldman in the Post Office this morning. We were both collecting our Social Security. Albert used to do a magic act round the clubs but a sudden attack of chronic arthritis forced his premature retirement last Christmas Eve at the Ivor Novello Miners Welfare Club.

Albert had reached the part of his act where he produced two live pigeons out of thin air. The pigeons waited patiently in the folds of his coat, their supply of oxygen fast running out, when Albert's fingers seized up. Albert tore feverishly at his coat with his stiffened digits, trying to release the gasping creatures but succeeding only in revealing layers of multi-coloured flags, ribbons and paper flowers which were to have formed the highlight of his second spot.

Panic set in. The audience cackled in cruel delight as they watched Albert, sweat dripping from his brow, tear open his shirt croaking 'I know they're in there somewhere'. Then, a few feathers fluttered into view and finally, the two half-suffocated pigeons thudded dazed to the floor.

Albert did not come out for his second spot after the Bingo. He was replaced by a Line and an extra Full House, his credibility shattered. It was the end of his professional career. Shortly afterwards he took a part-time job with the council as a relief gravedigger where he was on 24 hour stand-by in case an unforeseen plague struck the town and the regular man might have too much on his hands. He was never happy in the job, complaining that gravedigging offered little opportunity to join the Black Economy. 'You don't get many foreigners,' he used to grumble.

The queue in the Post Office shuffled forward.

"Still doing a bit, are you, Walter?" he asked me. A bit of *what* he omitted to say.

38

"Oh yes, Albert. Still doing a bit. And yourself?"

"Oh yes. Still doing a bit. Not as much as I did though."

"I heard you'd packed in the act. Arthritis wasn't it?"

"No it were not. That's just the malicious rumour my detractors put round. It were nothing like that." He paused. "I had Nervous Thumb if you must know."

"Nervous Thumb? Bit young for that aren't you?"

"I'm 73 next birthday."

"Precisely. I'm 84 and I've never had it."

"Just you wait. It'll get you in the end. It always does, Nervous Thumb."

"Put paid to your doings though, didn't it?"

"Not altogether. Like I say, I'm still doing a bit. On the side, like. In fact, I'm back on the boards tonight, Walter. Why don't you come down? I'm on the Compton Road Social and Welfare."

"Do you still do that trick where you saw a woman in half?"

"Sort of."

"What do you mean, *sort* of? Either you saw the bugger in half or you don't. Or do you leave her hanging by a thread, so to speak?"

"Don't be daft. No, it wore out didn't it? and I couldn't afford to buy it again on my pension. So I got the smaller version."

"You mean, you saw her in quarters?"

"No. Instead of sawing her in half, I saw her finger in two."

"Hey, that's a bit of a let down isn't it, Albert? Not much fun for the people at the back. They'll hardly be able to see it. Couldn't you saw it off and pass it round the audience and then stick it back on again?"

But he didn't take kindly to my suggestion. "Magic is about the art of illusion," he muttered haughtily, and moved forward to take his place at the grille. I noticed as he left that he'd put his pension book up his sleeve. Old habits die hard.

Jim Evans called round at teatime so I suggested we went down to the Welfare to watch him. "It might be good for a laugh," I said, so we arranged to get the 8 o'clock bus.

Word must have got round because the club was packed. The locals well remembered Albert's fiasco at the Ivor Novello and the place had the atmosphere of the Roman Coliseum.

Albert was on immediately after the pie and peas. He still wore the same dress suit I first recalled seeing at his Festival of Britain Show at the Town Hall, though it looked different in some way. I commented on this to Jim Evans.

"He's had it cleaned," pointed out Jim. "Those are different stains than

39

the ones he used to have. Don't you remember? For years he had the remains of the white sauce from the VE Night Christmas Party down his left lapel.

"So he did," I said. "I see there's a green blob there now."

"It's still steaming," observed Jim. "That must be his peas from tonight."

The first part of the act went well. Albert successfully produced his paper hankies, changed the colours of his flags and guessed correctly the suit of the playing card in his top hat, albeit at the fourth attempt. Then, at last, he reached his finale.

"Can I have a young lady volunteer from the audience?" he requested. There was no immediate response. Apart from the fact that nobody there was younger than 75, everybody remembered the fate of the choking pigeons. "There must be somebody," pleaded Albert.

Old Mrs Pemberton staggered to her feet and lurched towards the aisle.

"Christ, she's a game old bugger," said Jim. "I thought you told me she got burned to death at the Sunshine Club last month or were you exaggerating?"

We watched with mild interest as four willing hands guided Old Mrs Pemberton onto the stage.

"No, it was her cake that burned to death," I said. "But she had a stroke blowing the candles out. But she's had a dozen more since then—they don't seem to affect her. Mind you, she hardly knows what she's doing. She probably thinks she's going up there to collect her pension."

"What *is* she going up there for?"

"Albert's going to cut her finger off."

"Oh, is that all?"

"She won't miss it. Most of the rest of her's already been taken away at one time or another."

Albert took Old Mrs Pemberton's bony hands and held them up to the audience to demonstrate their completeness. "And now," he proclaimed grandly, "I am going to saw this lady's finger in half."

He produced the miniature guillotine that his meagre savings had been able to buy and placed the old crone's purple-veined finger between the razor-sharp blades. An expectant buzz was audible in the crowd. Dramatically, Albert released the small lever and the blade came down accompanied by a sharp howl from Old Mrs Pemberton and a spurt of blood which came to rest on Albert's lapel alongside the green pea stain.

"Oh Christ," groaned Albert.

The audience howled with laughter. "More!" they shouted. "Off with

40

her head," they cried.

"This isn't funny," shouted Albert. "She's bleeding."

"Who gets her finger?" shouted Little John Chapman. "Are you raffling it?"

"It's not funny," screamed Albert, as more of the pale, thin blood trickled from beneath the blades. "I don't know how it went wrong. It did it in rehearsal too. Is there a doctor in the club?"

"There's a doctor, but she's not in the club," roared Little John.

A retired District Nurse made her way to the stage and helped Old Mrs Pemberton to the wings, the guillotine still dangling from her finger.

"Don't forget to give it me back," Albert shouted after them. "I'm entitled to a refund. It was guaranteed."

"He's not going to do another, is he?" said Jim Evans.

"Why not?" I said. "They're shouting for more." And they were.

"Give us another," they chanted. "Who's next for Albert's Chopper?"

"I'd like to finish with my Bird Trick," announced Albert with as much dignity as he could summon under the circumstances. He opened a large box and dismantled the sides to show that it was completely empty. Then he reassembled it and put a black cloth over it before whispering a few magic words which nobody could hear but which Lily Ball, who is deaf and lipreads, later confirmed to be 'For God's sake let's get this over and a pint of Guinness inside me'.

"And now," cried Albert, ready for his moment of glory. "I give you—my box of tropical birds."

Triumphantly, he tore off the cloth and opened the box.

It was still empty. There was no sign of even one small feathered creature.

"Not a dicky bird," called out Little John Chapman.

"They must be here somewhere," shouted Albert in consternation. "It says so in the instructions."

Suddenly, from behind the box, a yellow budgerigar appeared and walked, rather than flew, to the front of the stage.

"He's clipped its wings," shouted Little John. "You'll have to get it a ladder to climb back up."

"I've not clipped its wings," retorted Albert. "It's the fumes from the glue that holds the box together. Makes them a bit drowsy."

"My God, glue-sniffing budgies. Do the RSPCA know about this?"

"Oh, the birds like it," said Albert innocently. "Makes them happy."

A second budgerigar, this time a blue one, joined its companion. The crowd cheered and started up 'You'll Never Walk Alone'. Within seconds, a dozen birds of every hue were tottering about the stage under the influence. Albert stepped forward in confusion, trod on a yellow one and fell over, nearly squashing three more with his ample bottom.

"Go on, Albert. You nearly got them that time. Have another go."

"Shame," shouted Mrs Hargreaves. "Animal Aid should be informed. Boooo." Hissing and booing followed as the mood turned ugly but good humour was restored when three birds hopped on to Albert's head and relieved themselves in his sparse hair. Another did the same on his dress suit lapel, leaving its white mark next to the green pea stain and light crimson of Old Mrs Pemberton's blood.

"A blessing he doesn't use seagulls," commented Mrs Hargreaves, as the curtain was hastily drawn and Albert Gouldman's career finally came to an end.

He joined us at the bar later. "My Nervous Thumb, Walter," he said. "But I'm not letting it beat me. I'm going to have to give up the magic, of course, but I thought I might have a go at singing. I've been taking secret yodelling lessons. Do you want to hear me?"

"I think it's time we were off," I said to Jim Evans. "I'm too old for experiences like that at 84."

THURS JAN 24TH

Dramatic news! Neville has got a mistress!

And Marge has found out!

It didn't take much detective work on Marge's part. The mistress had thoughtfully left a message on their telephone answering machine.

When I arrived there with my washing, they had just returned from Nottingham with Natalie who had been fined £50 in the Magistrates Court for obstructing the police in the execution of their duty. She had lain in the road in the path of an oncoming police Rover shouting "Go on, run me down you Fascist pigs".

Had I been the driver of the Rover, I would have happily acceded to her request but the policeman merely alighted, dragged her to the gutter by her long, unwashed hair and arrested her. An ignominious end to her crusade and a source of embarrassment to Neville should it ever get out at the Conservative Club.

But . . . nothing compared to the embarrassment he faced when Marge played back the messasge on the Ansaphone.

"Hello sexy," breathed a husky female voice. "You were great last night. You made bells ring for me." Marge listened open-mouthed. "I can't

43

believe you're really 39."

"He's not, he's over 50," shouted Marge at the machine.

"Bells?" I said. "Is she referring to Evensong at the Mussolini Avenue Methodist Church?"

"I beg your pardon." Neville entered the room having locked up the car. He had all the nonchalance of a man who is unaware the world is about to explode in his face. Relentlessly, the voice continued.

"I hope you can make it on Saturday, Nev. Why don't you tell her you're going to the Party Conference then we could have a week together. She'll never know it's in October."

Marge switched off the machine in fury and confronted her husband who stood before her red-faced, open-mouthed and a likely candidate for an instant coronary.

"Stay here, you worm," barked Marge. "I'm going to search your pockets for further evidence."

In his wallet, Marge found a picture of a stranger inscribed 'To my Nevsy, Love Edna'. The stranger was a woman of Joan Collins' age but bearing more resemblance to Irene Handl. This seemed to upset Marge even more.

"Couldn't you get anything better than that old bag?" she shouted. "If you had to have a mistress you didn't have to pick an ugly one. How do you think it makes me look to be thrown over for THAT."

"You've got it wrong," protested Neville. "Edna is from the Conservative Club. We share a common interest in the climb to power of the Tory Wets. She only regards me as another member."

"She must be easily satisfied if it's only your member she's interested in."

Natalie remained aloof from the argument, saying she preferred to concentrate on the real issues of the times like Greenham Common and the Workers' Battle. This latter I took to mean Arthur Scargill's attempts to swell the unemployment figures by losing the miners their jobs in the hope the Government would get the blame for the appalling employment statistics.

"I have no time for trivial matters," she declared archly.

"It was through these 'trivial matters' you got here," stormed Marge angrily but Natalie merely snorted. Marge picked up her handbag. "I'm coming to live with you, Dad."

I shuddered. The thought of Marge's Spotted Dick following me across town was too much. "It's a men's hostel," I lied. "No women allowed. Anyway, what would Neville do without you?"

44

The flesh wobbled on Marge's bones. She was wearing a blue spotted dress that Neville had bought her three Christmasses ago and she resembled a giant bean bag.

"You're right," she agreed. "Why should I allow him to make another woman's life a misery. I owe it to this trollop to stay and put him on the right track."

Neville interrupted the conversation. "This phone call is just a joke," he insisted. "A fellow at work has got his wife to ring up for a laugh."

"And what about the photo? How do you explain that?"

Neville had no answer. As the background was the Conservative Club and she wore a digital watch on her wrist, he could hardly pass her off as a French peasant he had rescued under heavy gunfire in Brittany in 1944.

Marge went to spend the night with her friend Kath Lloyd, an anaemic Welsh girl who advised her to withold her favours from Neville as a punishment in the manner of the Ancient Roman women. However, Marge decided that this would probably be a relief to Neville who was never a vigorous man, so she determined to pursue the opposite course and force him to perform his marital duties twice nightly until further notice with no time off for headaches or faked impotence.

I don't envy Neville's future lot. Certainly I shall never marry again. Five times is enough. At 84, I shall be content to enjoy a succession of young lovers without giving in to their inevitable demands for matrimony.

FRI JAN 25TH

Big shock this morning. Natalie, of all people, arrived at my flat after breakfast complete with two suitcases and a machine like a portable electro-cardiograph which she referred to as her ghetto blaster.

"I've decided to move in with you, Walter," she announced. "The atmosphere couldn't be worse at home if Neville had been found in bed with Larry Grayson."

"How are your father and mother?" I enquired solicitously.

"Not speaking. She's convinced he's got harlots hidden all over town that she hasn't found out about yet. It amazes me how he ever got a mistress at all at his age. He's fifty you know."

"I should know. I made him." I did not care for the implications here. If a man 34 years my junior was written off as a sexual cripple, what chance was there of me convincing women that I was still in my virile prime.

"It's all right then, if I move in for a bit?" She had already hung up several garments in the wardrobe.

"Why not?" This could greatly enhance my status in the house. Everyone would assume Gnat was my lover thus establishing my reputation as a Great Lover in the Errol Flynn mould.

When she had finished unpacking, she switched on the ghetto blaster, filling the room with a noise which shook the walls and rattled the cutlery. "Peter and The Test Tube Babies," she said. "Great, aren't they?" I switched down my hearing aid.

Natalie rifled through her anorak pockets and produced a cigarette machine. "We had those in the War," I shouted, watching her insert the paper and the shreds of what I assumed was tobacco.

"Never tasting like these I'll bet. Here, try one." She licked and closed the paper and handed me the finished cigarette. I lit it and took in a mouthful of sweet acrid smoke.

"I think it makes me feel happy," I boomed, still competing with The Test Tube Babies and Peter. I took another drag.

"All right, that's enough for now, Walter. Can't have you feeling happy at this time of the morning." She snatched it back and sucked in deeply. "Right! I've got all my stuff in. I'll be back later."

"Hang on. Do you want me to get you some dinner? Only on my pension . . ."

"I won't be wanting dinner, Walter. You just carry on as if I wasn't here. I don't imagine I'll be back till very late tonight." Picking up her ghetto blaster, she flounced out.

She was not back for dinner. I ate my bean rissole alone and then settled down to an evening of black and white television. Unfortunately, it was snooker and I had difficulty in following the play.

By 11 o'clock, there was no sign of Gnat so I assumed she'd gone back to Marge and Neville's after all and I went to bed.

At 3 a.m., I was wakened by a crowd of people pouring into the flat. At first I thought it was Russian invaders until I recognised Gnat in the middle of the melee, shouting and waving a bottle of cheap Italian wine.

"Didn't wake you up did we, Walter?" she cried happily.

Beneath the covers, I smoothed my nightshirt over my knees. "Oh no. As a matter of fact I was thinking of getting up to do a bit of spring cleaning."

Sarcasm was wasted on my grand-daughter. "I've brought back a few friends for you to meet."

"Really? Miners, are they?"

"No, they're from college."

"Ah, minors!"

"I just said, they're from college." I gave up. "Do you want a blow?" she asked.

46

"A blow what?"

"It's slang for joint, Walter."

"It's three in the morning," I said. "And I had my dinner at six. This is no time to start cooking. When are these people going?"

She switched on the ghetto blaster. "Going? They've only just arrived. Here, take a swig of this instead." She passed over the bottle of wine and I took a swig. "Take it," she offered. "We've got plenty."

I don't remember much more.

SAT JAN 26TH

Awoke at noon feeling very dizzy with a dry throat, splitting headache and an empty bottle of Italian wine lodged beneath my nightshirt. A cloud of stale smoke hung over the room like a dead genie and the floor was littered with empty bottles and cigarette butts. Lying on the carpet between patches of drying vomit was Gnat, locked in the arms of a large black man with Rastafarian locks and an earring. He was stark naked.

I staggered out of bed and prodded them with my bare feet. The black man shot up, took one look at me and screamed. "God Almighty, Marley's Ghost."

Natalie stirred, turned over and rubbed her eyes until they opened. She wore only a pair of minute pink knickers and a T-shirt bearing the inscription 'Help Stamp Out Aids—Kill A Queer'. "Oh, it's you, Walter. What time is it?" She turned to her companion who was still staring at me in horror. "What's the matter with you?" she demanded. "You've gone quite pale."

Only the palms of his hands, I thought.

"Walter," said Natalie. "I'd like you to meet Harold Wilson. Harold's got a degree in Japanese History but thanks to the inhuman policies of a capitalist government he works as a self-employed window cleaner in Neasden."

"Perhaps if Mrs Thatcher were to open a chain of Japanese museums throughout North London, he might be better catered for."

"That's right," smiled Harold Wilson. "Lots more windows for me to clean. There's better money in windows." He ignored Natalie's withering glance.

"I'd like you to meet my grandfather," she said. "Walter Sherlock. He's 96."

"I'd like some breakfast," I said. "Two Shredded Wheats and hot milk."

"I'll get it," said Natalie and waltzed off to the kitchen. She returned

47

some minutes later with the bowl, placed it on the table in front of me and switched on the ghetto blaster.

"Breakfast OK Walter?" she shouted.

"As a matter of fact," I shouted back, "it's horrible. The worst thing I've tasted since your mother's Spotted Dick."

"Hang on." Natalie looked puzzled and ran into the kitchen. "Sorry about that, Walter," she said, returning with a new dish. "It looked just like Shredded Wheat."

I looked down at the tangled shreds I had been eating. "What was it?" I asked querulously.

Harold Wilson broke into a loud Zambian guffaw. "Hashish, man. You've had hashish for yo' breakfast."

I slept intermittently for the rest of the day and had strange dreams in which Neil Kinnock, dressed as Odille in 'Swan Lake', was arrested for selling automatic umbrellas in Oxford Street without a street trader's licence. He was sentenced to watch 'The Mousetrap' for 72 consecutive days.

When I finally staggered to my feet at six the next morning, Natalie had taken all her things and left. A short note on the sideboard informed me that she was taking up residence with Harold Wilson. He needed someone to hold his bucket.

SUN JAN 27TH

It took me all day to straighten the flat after the Natalie Occupation and two hours of this was sorting out the *real* Shredded Wheats.

I had intended to go to Evensong at the Elim Pentecostal Revival Hall but my ankle was playing me up as it always does in wet weather.

The original injury was sustained some years ago when I twisted it in a pothole in Emmanuel Shinwell Boulevard. I naturally sued the Corporation for £700,000 damages, pointing out that the disability would severely handicap my chances of success in the New York Marathon which I had been hoping to win that year.

They said that, at 77, the injury could be a blessing in disguise. They did not hold out much hope of my finishing the New York Marathon at all, even in my original pristine condition and allowing two years for the journey.

Eventually, an independent tribunal awarded me £125 and a pink badge which entitled me to park anywhere in the town centre free of charge. The only problem then was learning to drive with one eye.

The lasting effect from the injury concerned my digestive system. In falling over the pothole, I twisted a muscle in my upper thigh. Subsequently, when passing wind, I have never been able to give that little twist of the bottom so necessary to ensure a lusty and successful expulsion of air.

This inability has been further aggravated by my macrobiotic diet which produces excessive flatulence.

Dr Gavin says I am the only person in town registered disabled because of my inability to fart in time.

MON JAN 28TH

Recovered from my enforced drug addiction, I went round to Marge and Neville's to see if hostilities had ceased or if they'd killed one another. Only Marge was in and she was in a belligerent mood.

"All this living on your own at your age is ridiculous. Look at you, you look like you're wasting away."

I tried to explain that my lean, athletic appearance was caused by my healthy macrobiotic diet but she continued unabated.

"And those awful clothes you're wearing. Gladstone used to wear a coat like that. You must be the only person in the country with button-up flies and it wouldn't be so bad if you had all the buttons. What's wrong with zips, that's what I'd like to know."

"Bloke I knew had a nasty accident with a zip. Lethal as a bacon slicer they can be. Nearly cut his . . ."

"All right. I don't care to know about that. It's about time you moved into the 1980's. I'm taking you into town. Neville can buy you some new clothes. You are his father." She produced Neville's wallet from her apron pocket. "Good job he left this behind," she said maliciously.

I was taken to a gent's outfitters in Goebbels Street where my clothes were pulled off me and I had to try on a succession of brown tweed jackets and cavalry twill trousers.

"These are the sort of dull, modern clothes a man of your age should wear." I nodded obediently. Marge eventually chose a dun jacket with leather elbow patches. "This should last a good twenty years," she said. "It'll do for Neville after your funeral."

The trousers she picked were a diarrhoea coloured check made of material akin to horsehair.

"These'll be itchy," I protested.

"You won't notice them over your combinations. Now we must get you some shoes. Those elastic sided galoshes don't look as if they'll last out the week."

49

"They've lasted since the War," I told her. "I've little reason to doubt they'll be around when hostilities start up again."

Marge took no notice. I was equipped with a pair of brown brogues with thick rubber soles which would have been ideal for trekking through rivers but out of place in the drawing rooms of the affluent society. I pointed this out to Marge but she said most of the people I knew belonged rather to the effluent society, well suited to boots such as those.

Finally, my cherished bowler was replaced by a piece of headgear once the sole province of the Alpine yodeller—complete with feather.

"Very smart," approved Marge, leading me to the shop mirror.

"I look like a pillock," I protested but to no avail. "He'll keep these on," she said. "Pack his other stuff up, I'll take it to Oxfam."

Which is where I got most of it in the first place.

TUES JAN 29TH

Natalie appeared at the flat this morning with Harold Wilson in tow. She looked at my new clothes in horror. "Whatever have you got on, Walter?"

"Your mother took me shopping yesterday," I explained mournfully.

"But you look dreadful."

"She said I looked dreadful the way I was before. She said I was a relic of the Hansom Cab Age when the country was plagued by the twin threats of Napoleon and mounting horse manure in the streets."

"So she bought you some trousers to match it."

"Please, who is this Napoleon?" enquired Harold Wilson.

Natalie ignored him. "You're coming with us, Walter. I'll get you properly dressed, if you must go modern. Personally, I thought your Disraeli Look was quintessentially you."

"As a matter of fact, I was just on my way to Oxfam to recover my old things."

"Wonderful. We'll take you down. I've got the car outside."

I looked out of the window and spied Marge's Robin Reliant dwarfed by the telephone kiosk.

"I'm getting a roof rack for it," said Natalie, "for the next time we go camping."

"I'll save you some bones from my salmon steak at tea-time," I said. "They should just reach across."

"Oh, very funny," snapped Gnat. Harold Wilson emitted one of his guffaws which she silenced with a withering glance.

"I knew a bloke who used to help make those cars. He was an aero dynamics tester. His job was to blow them down the wind-tunnel with his blowpipe."

"As a matter of fact," said Natalie icily, "this is my car now. Marge has made Neville buy her a new one. It's the start of his penance."

"He's set a dangerous precedent there. She'll soak him dry in no time."

"It's his own fault for being so stupid as to get caught. Marge won't be so careless."

"Marge?" I said quickly. "You don't mean . . .?"

"Marge has become very friendly with Harold's step-father." Harold Wilson had the grace to blush, not easy for a man of his hue.

"Has this colonial relationship been going on long?"

"Oh no. Only since Marge found out about Neville's shameful infidelity."

"Is she very fond of Harold's step-father?"

"Oh, not at all. She only goes with him because he's got Marxist tendencies so she knows it will upset Neville."

"But she only found out about Neville last Thursday. How long has she been philandering with this Leftie?"

"Since Sunday teatime. So far, they've only been out once; to the Trotskyites Against Nuclear Fission Rally at Sellafield."

This was grave news. Neville's whole position could be undermined. Before I could remonstrate with Gnat, she hurried me out to the car and took me to her idea of a suitable clothes shop. Even the window dummies had Mohican haircuts.

"Have you got any money, Walter?"

"Only my pension I got last Wednesday. I think there's about 70p left."

"Better hand it over anyway."

"But my dinner and tea today?"

"We'll worry about that later. I'm going to have to lend you some as it is. Good job I've got Neville's Barclaycard."

The shop was not my idea of a gent's outfitters. Pop music blared out of strategically placed speakers and flashing coloured lights changed the shades of the clothes every two seconds.

"The shops are self-service nowadays because the assistants can't make themselves heard above the noise," explained Natalie. Harold Wilson, meanwhile, had disappeared.

My new outfit bore little resemblance to either of my previous styles. I tried to tell Natalie that, at 84, a red and grey anorak, purple sweater, yellow canvas trousers and green knitted shirt did not go with my sparse grey hair, National Health deaf-aid and brown brogue boots. Her answer

51

was to add a pair of maroon moccasins to my new wardrobe.

"I look like a decorated totem pole," I protested.

"Nonsense, you look wonderful, Walter. A touch of the Quentin Crisps."

At that moment we were rejoined by Harold Wilson carrying a large brown bag. "I've just been to get a few things for myself," he explained, "down the road."

Just as I suspected. He'd been to Oxfam and bought up all my old gear.

"The bowler suits you, Harold," approved Gnat.

"What about me?"

"You'll be glad of your anorak in these icy winter winds," said Natalie. "Don't be so ungrateful."

So now I have two outfits, both hideous in their own way. When I've saved up enough from my pension, I'll be off to the Red Cross shop to get dressed properly again.

WED JAN 30TH

I met old Jacob Dickins on the No. 7 bus into town this morning. He was the object of some attention on the lower deck owing to the unpleasant smell emanating from his person. I commented on this.

"You pong a bit today, Jacob," I said.

"It's coming from the inside of my trousers, Walter. I've got this infection." A lady sitting in front of us alighted early.

"It's not Aids is it?" I enquired nervously. This Aids is a complaint that could put the blight on my late flowering in the Permissive Society with the headlong rush back to virginity being all the rage amongst middle aged women in our part of the world.

"Don't be daft. It's termites."

"Those little red insects that hens get, you mean?"

"Something like that. Only they're in my leg; eating it away." He tapped his left knee.

"Have you been to the doctor's?"

"Bugger the doctor," said Jacob. "All that messing around in germ-ridden waiting rooms with those insolent receptionists glaring at you. No, I went to the garden centre instead. They fixed me up nicely."

"Hang on, your left leg. Isn't that the one that got shot off in the War?"

"Exactly. This is my wooden one. What you can smell is the creosote they put on it, to kill the termites."

"Not good for social life though, Jacob."

"I don't do so badly, Walter. Not for 76. I'm in one of them Amateur

Dramatic groups, you know, at the Denis Compton Avenue United Reform Church."

"The one where the defrocked Methodists go?"

"That's the one. They have this group—the North End Players."

"Do you get good parts?"

"Mainly butlers so far. You see, I can't learn too many lines since I got my cataracts so they usually keep me down to 'dinner is served on the balcony, Sir James'. I say that a lot, whatever the play. Why don't you come along, Walter? There's a few nice women there."

"Brigitte Bardot types?"

"Well no. More like Dandy Nichols but they're game sorts if you take my meaning."

"If they can clamber out of their wheelchairs, eh Jacob?"

"Well, what can you expect at our age?"

"I can expect women of youth and classical beauty," I said haughtily.

"Really?" Jacob Dickins did not seem impressed. "Anyway, it's Play Selection night tonight. Why don't you come along and see for yourself? You could even put in for a part if you fancy it."

I'd nothing else on so I agreed. I splashed most of my pension buying a decent shirt with a Gladstonian wing collar from Dr Barnardo's and a musty bowler from the Red Cross.

Feeling more like my old self after yesterday's shopping fiasco, I turned up at the Church Hall at eight o'clock.

"He's a friend of mine," explained Jacob to the Chairlady of the Selection Committee. "And he's very keen to act, aren't you, Walter?"

I nodded silently, Clint Eastwood style.

"We don't need any more butlers," said the woman, icily. "We have a job fitting them into every play to accommodate Jacob here."

"I have no wish to be a butler, madam," I retorted haughtily. "I was thinking more in terms of the romantic lead."

She let out a discordant bellow that would not have disgraced a yak. "Romantic lead! At your age! My God, the man's ninety if he's a day."

"Nothing that a clever make up department couldn't handle. The bone structure's still there you know."

"And what part were you thinking of? Lord Rochester perhaps? Something classical. Or perhaps Richard the Third? More your shape. Or even Oliver Twist."

"Excuse me, Gloria." The interruption came from a pale man with shiny knees on his trousers. "You could let him be in 'Waiting for Godot'."

"Not as a butler," I said suspiciously.

53

"Oh no dearie, the lead role. You could be Godot."

She smiled serenely. "Oh yes, perfect Ernest. The title role. You'd like that wouldn't you?"

"Take no notice, Walter," said Jacob. "They're having you on. Godot; he's the bugger what never comes on. You'd never set foot on the stage."

"Ah no, but he'd be there in the wings wouldn't he?" said the woman.

"Waiting," added Ernest.

"Keeping the audience in suspense, wondering if you are ever going to arrive."

"But they don't see me?"

"Well, they couldn't, could they? I mean, if they could see you, it wouldn't be 'Waiting for Godot' would it? It would be 'Godot Waiting for Them'. And they'd be there already anyway." She stopped, confused.

"I can do impressions," I ventured. "Would you like to see Lord Attlee?"

"Nobody in our audience will remember Lord Attlee," said Gloria tartly.

"Course they will," said Jacob, sticking up for me. "He was a fast bowler for Essex. Black fellow with enormous hands."

Gloria ignored him. "The play we expect to choose is Somerset Maugham's 'The Constant Wife'. And there is no place in it for a Lord Attlee, black or otherwise."

"Why don't you fix him up with a place in Wardrobe?" suggested Ernest.

This sounded like a better idea. I could be the one helping the leading lady out of her glamorous costume.

"Have you had any experience of dressing?" enquired Gloria.

I was tempted to tell her that my experience had been more in Undressing and that I hoped to do more of it, but the look on her face stopped me.

Another lady joined the fray, an obvious rival to the Chairlady. "Some of us are in favour of a revue type show for the next production. You know, musical and dramatic sketches. Mr Clackitt wants to do his Hinge and Bracket piece but Mrs Clackitt is not so keen because, on the last occasion, he took down their living room curtains for the costumes."

"I can do Norman Evans," I ventured. "Over the garden wall, remember? I take my teeth out and wear a woman's apron."

"That should excite some of the older women in the audience," murmured the Chairlady, sarcastically. "Particularly the deaf and blind ones."

The discussion was interrupted by tea and biscuits. The tea was beige coloured and poured from a gigantic, verdigrised urn that looked suspiciously like the open end of a trombone inexpertly sealed by low grade welders. The biscuits were soft.

At the end of the evening, a vote was taken to decide the play. The choice was 'The Constant Wife'. Jacob was selected to play the butler. I was placed in charge of the urn. Tomorrow I shall buy some Brasso.

THURS JAN 31ST

I have decided to cast my net wider in search of a new partner. Quite obviously I am having no success in this town, word having got round about the unfortunate incident with Mrs Washington and my replacement hair.

So, today, I filled in an application form to join a Computer Dating Company. For £25, they supply you with the names and addresses of six women, selected to your personal specification. A sort of crumpet by mail order.

The application forms were slightly longer and more complicated than an entry visa to tour the Kremlin and needed careful study, so I took them with me when I went to meet Jim Evans for our morning cup of tea at the Casualty Department of the Otis Redding Memorial Hospital.

"I don't like coming here, Walter," moaned Jim. "I keep thinking someone in a white coat is going to come in and operate on me."

"It's the cheapest tea in town," I pointed out, "all made by volunteers. Besides, those women in WRVS uniforms get me very excited. They remind me of my adventures in the air raid shelters in 1946."

"But the War ended in 1945."

"Precisely. So the shelters were empty in 1946. I had some rare old times in them." I handed across the forms. "Here. See what you make of those."

He peered at them closely through his sellotaped spectacles and looked up, shocked. "You're not advertising for a woman?"

"More like buying one, Jim. And, come to think of it, it might do you some good to do the same, the lamentable record of seduction you've had in recent times. It's 16 years to my knowledge since you've had a woman other than Mrs Evans."

"It's 16 years since I've had Mrs Evans. She says women lose all interest in those matters once they've had half their organs removed. The trouble is, the only organ I can recall her losing was an impacted wisdom tooth in 1973."

"That's it then. Get one of these yourself and you could have a nice 25 year old girl in time for Easter."

"Would I hold much appeal, though, for a girl of 25?"

"If you kept your teeth in and didn't reveal any portion of your naked body except in pitch darkness."

"I'll have you know I've got the body of a man of twenty," protested Jim Evans, indignantly. "At least, down to the bottom button of my vest." He scrutinised my application form. "I see you haven't revealed your great age."

"I've ticked the box marked 'over 40'. They don't go above that."

"Perhaps you should give them a bit of a clue, though. You could add WELL over 40. And what's all this? You've put here that you earn £20,000 plus a year, you're six foot tall, above average intelligence and Jewish. Have you been circumcised then?"

"Only once. In South Shields in 1926."

"Won't these women get a shock when they're expecting Omar Sharif and you turn up?"

"Only for a split second. Then my natural charm and animal magnetism will win them over."

"And failing that, they'll set their guide dogs on you."

"Be serious, Jim. I want you to help me with the rest of this form. It's not an easy job, this. For example, this question here, 'Do you want your partner to be sexually experienced or a virgin?' "

"Oh yes, both of those," nodded Jim Evans.

"How can she be experienced and a virgin, you dolt?"

"Easy. She can have read a lot about it but be untouched by human hand."

"Full of unawakened lust, you mean? Yes, I'll go along with that. Now, what about religion? There's plenty to choose from—Catholic, Buddhist, C of E, Quaker, Moslem . . ."

"Just put 'no'," advised Jim. "No sense in attracting Bible thumpers and celibates. Stick to your own kind—rampaging Non-Believers."

"Next—musical tastes. I don't like women that whistle a lot. Especially if they have bad breath and most of them do."

"Yes. It comes from all that heavy breathing they do."

"I'll put non-musical then."

It took us another hour to complete the forms by which time I had established that I was looking for girls who were white, single, well-groomed, non-smokers, atheists, under 20 and heirs to medium-sized fortunes. And preferably existing on macrobiotic diets.

"Nothing untoward about those requirements," said Jim Evans as I sealed the envelope. "They'll be queueing at your door this time next week."

By which time, the episode with Mrs Washington will be a forgotten nightmare.

FRI FEB 1ST

Out of the blue, I got a letter from the Job Centre asking if I would like to do some Market Research, one morning a week. They are recruiting pensioners to roam the streets asking passers-by personal questions about their feet.

I went along after breakfast to sign up. I start next Thursday.

But the most important event of the day occurred in the Tea and Crumpet tearooms in the High Street.

I fell in love.

Because of the January Sales in Debenhams, which have started in February this year to help build up the suspense, the tables were crowded. I was thus forced to share my usual table in the inglenook with a stranger— a lady with aristocratic features and a purple hat.

She introduced herself as Mrs Miley and offered me a slice of her wholemeal scone. She is bereft of a partner, her husband having been garotted by German parachutists in the Normandy campaign. She has not, so far, replaced him, contenting herself, instead, with the company of a neutered bitch called Wilfred.

I told her that I, too, had lost the companionship of my previous wives through differing circumstances which were no fault of my own, and she coyly patted my hand through the thick wool of my mittens.

Plucking up courage, I asked her if she would care to accompany me to the Holy Mother of Mary Over 60's Night on Sunday and she accepted.

Before we parted, I asked her for a photograph. The only one she had with her was a newspaper cutting from 1950 depicting a fire in a fish and chip shop in Eisenhower Street. She is not at her best, being one of those being dragged from the inferno by heroic firemen.

I shall keep it in my wallet next to my other prized possessions—my identity card, my membership to the All India Bingo Club, my bus pass and a form giving doctors the right to remove my vital organs for research if I am run over by a No. 27 bus.

Until Sunday then.

What sort of flowers should I take her? Perhaps a single orchid. Or maybe a dozen red roses. What a calamity that I spent most of my pension on new clothes yesterday, although it was probably the wing collar that attracted Mrs Miley.

SAT FEB 2ND

Decided to go to the doctor's this morning to get my eyes tested. As usual, the surgery was full and conditions in the waiting room were very unpleasant with people coughing and sneezing when they should have been in bed.

"Hello, Mr Sherlock," said the receptionist. "We haven't seen you for a long time; let me see, it must be at least a fortnight now. Have you been on holiday?"

I ignored the heavy sarcasm. "You ought to have a separate waiting room for people who aren't ill," I said, indicating the disease-ridden multitude I was expected to join. "You never know what you might catch going in with that lot."

"People who aren't ill don't usually come here," she pointed out. "We're not a snooker hall, you know, and the doctor has given up the Spanish guitar lessons."

I persisted. "All the same, you should segregate the people with infectious complaints."

"I'm sure if we had bigger premises, Mr Sherlock, we would do just that. We could have a Measles Room, an Influenza Room and maybe a passage for malaria sufferers as they aren't so prevalent in this district. Of course, if you were unable to make a quick self-diagnosis before you got here, you would have to form part of the Mystery Queue, lumped in with the other indecisives who were not sure whether they had tonsilitis or Aids. And imagine the disappointment in finding out you'd only got a streptococcic throat and you'd been cooped up for two hours with the victims of Legionnaires Disease. I think you are better off the way you are. Your eyes did you say?"

I blinked. I swear she never drew breath. Had I not seen her lips move I'd have taken her for an answering machine.

"I want some glasses," I said.

"Going blind are you?" she asked suspiciously. "What have you been doing?"

"I'm not discussing my recreational habits with you," I replied. "Just get me in that surgery. I'm too old to stand at 84."

"I'll get you a commode, if you like."

I sat on a wooden chair nearest the door, hoping to catch lungfuls of new air before it got contaminated. On the table beside me were the same copies of Taxation and Mechanical Engineering that had been there on my previous seventy three visits, both dated 1981.

"It's my leg," said the lady next to me, suddenly and without introduction.

"I beg your pardon."

"Only I can't move it from the ankle down."

I glanced down at the offending foot. "It's in plaster of Paris, that's why."

"No it isn't. That's my surgical stocking to help my circulation. I'm sorry if it's in your way."

"That's a big leg you've got there," I said. "Elephantiasis, I shouldn't wonder."

"Oh no. It's 'cos I've got six layers of bandages on. I suffer from varicose veins."

"You can die with those," I told her. "It only needs one clot of blood to swim up to your heart and within seconds you're a stiff."

She paled. "The doctor never told me that."

"He probably didn't like to worry you. But I think it's better to know these things. Gives you time to get your affairs settled before you're taken. You have made your will, I take it?"

"No, I haven't. Should I?" She looked frightened.

"As soon as you're out of here. In fact, I'd make it before you go in. One examination from Burke and Hare in there could easily start the ball rolling. I'd get down to see your solicitor. I'll save your place in here."

She scuttled out of the door and I moved into her seat. "Next," cried the receptionist.

I jumped up quickly. "I'm 84," I shouted to the other patients. "I've come about my father, he needs urgent treatment," and before anyone could move I was through the door and into the surgery.

"Not you again," Dr Gavin greeted me.

"My sentiments entirely," I replied. "Why can't I have a brown doctor like everyone else?"

"Dr Patel is on evening duty this week. What's the trouble, Mr Sherlock?"

"I want my eyes tested."

"The opticians will do that, free of charge."

"I want the experts. No shopgirl plays around with my pupils."

"That's what my old Housemaster used to say. Now then, stand on that white line and read the bottom line of that notice hung on the wall."

I squinted across the room. "Made in Hong Kong."

"The bottom line, I said."

"That IS the bottom line. Underneath GSHDL."

He walked across, took out a magnifying glass and read the tiny letters. "My God, so it is. You've got perfect vision. What do you want glasses for?"

"I want a pair of tinted ones to match my suntan."

"Mr Sherlock; your suntan, as you call it, is bordering on alabaster. I laid someone out this morning who was less pale than you. If I didn't know you'd already had three pints since Christmas, I'd be sending you for a blood transfusion."

"Ah but I'm going on this sunbed this afternoon and I've got this vinegar mixture to spread all over me, a recipe an old gypsy gave me."

"One whose palm you failed to cross with silver I presume. Well that should give you a distinctive aroma if nothing else. Now, if you'll excuse me, I've got genuine patients to see."

"What about my glasses? I'm looking for the Michael Caine effect."

"The optician will sell you a frame with plain glass in. Thank you for calling."

"I'll see you on Monday then."

"Monday?"

"For my wart ointment. I'm running low."

"Wait a minute. I'll give you a prescription for a barrelfull and then you needn't call again until Christmas."

You think he'd welcome regular customers, all contributing to his nice little earner from the NHS.

I might join BUPA. That would show him.

In the end, I decided against glasses. They might interfere with the alignment of my wig.

SUN FEB 3RD

The preparation for my first night out with Mrs Miley did not go too well. Dr Gavin's warnings about the sunbed treatment and my Romany potion were well-founded. Far from tanning me an even bronze, it left dark, ugly stains on my person plus a lingering odour which attracted all the cats in the neighbourhood.

Furthermore, when I tried to scrub the marks off, more of them stuck to the side of the bath. Mrs Newfoundland thought they were oil slicks and notified the landlord to send for BP but, after a quick inspection, Mr Murray decided the problem was creeping rust. However, he declared himself unable to afford a new one due to the crippling effect of the 1980 Rent Act so Ron Alley is organising a Residents' Appeal to buy a replacement suite. A red thermometer is to be painted on the hall wall to indicate progress of contributions.

There was bad news, too, about my wig. There must have been a leak at the back of the airing cupboard that caused the damp but, whatever the reason, the wig had gone mouldy and looked like a rotting shrew. Smelt like one too.

Luckily I had my new bowler, though I wish the woman at the Red Cross had not written 50p across the brim in white chalk. I tried to ink it out the best I could but it still showed through in a certain light.

Having spent nearly all my pension on my new finery, I was unable to afford the bouquet of flowers I had intended taking to Mrs Miley. Instead, after tea when dusk had fallen, I crept through a gap in the hedge surrounding the Bob Geldof Municipal Park and picked what I could. Mainly snowdrops and hawthorn berries. Luckily, I had a medium packet of Smarties left over from Christmas and still in their Cellophane, so I ironed an old Harrods bag and took them along with the flowers wrapped in that.

We met in the bus shelter in the Market. All the glass had been smashed and the wind howled through. "I'm frozen," Mrs Miley greeted me. "You're 20 minutes late. I thought you'd passed away in the meantime."

I reassured her of my continued existence, explaining that the No. 27 bus had been held up by stone-throwing vandals as it passed the Depot.

"Children, was it?" enquired Mrs Miley.

"No. Striking bus conductors. Luckily, we got a scab driver or I wouldn't be here now."

"Never mind, there was plenty to read on the shelter." She indicated the aerosol-sprayed graffiti: 'Jesus Saves—but not with the Halifax' and 'Will somebody tell Baggy Bruford about Durex'.

"Very tasteful," I murmured, taking her hand as we walked the two hundred yards to the Over 60's. Jim Evans was in, sporting the family dentures. It occurred to me I might get a few extra teeth myself. The one solitary occupant of my bottom gum is situated off-centre which gives me a look of Quasimodo on the rare occasions I break into a smile.

"Has she got a friend, then?" asked Jim as I joined him at the bar to get the halves of stout in.

"Yes, but it's called Wilfred and bites your feet in the night. I don't know why you don't have a go at Mrs Washington. One night with her would keep you going until your Golden Wedding."

During the Housey, I allowed my hand to brush casually against the knee of her surgical stocking. "Not here," she whispered, crossing off 32 on her card.

"Where then?" I cried excitedly but the question went unanswered.

After the last house we had the strict tempo dancing with the Rodney Stuart Quintet. This was mny chance to get a closer grip. I slid my knee gently between hers as we swayed to the Veleta. "You may call me Walter," I whispered invitingly.

"You can call me Queenie," she replied, squeezing my hand in a gesture of spontaneous lust.

"And you can call *me* anytime." It was Big Barry, terror of the Over 60's jam-making class, six foot two without his caliper. "This is a ladies excuse me, I believe."

Before I could explain to him it was the ladies who were meant to do the excusing, he kneed me aside with a glancing blow to the groin and swooped off with Mrs Miley. I was left staggering against the wall and was condemned to watch him limping across the dance floor with her through the foxtrot, the Dashing White Sergeant and the Eva Three Step.

Fortune smiled my way, however, as we came up to the last waltz. Big Barry was suddenly seized by one of his recurrent angina attacks. As he slumped to the ground clutching his bottle of emergency yellow tablets, I kicked him aside and took the lady back in my arms.

"I like a purposeful man, Walter," she smiled as we glided away from the recumbent form of her recent partner, now frothing at the mouth like a porpoise out of water.

I narrowed my eyes like Humphrey Bogart and slid my hands from her shoulders down to the upper rim of her whalebone corsets. She squirmed girlishly in my grasp. I pressed my lips to hers and felt her tongue playfully pushing into my mouth, its tip flicking my bottom tooth to and fro in time to the music.

"How do you fancy a weekend away?" I asked heavily, as we paused for breath. "Just the two of us."

"The three of us you mean, Walter."

My mind went back to Big Barry who was now rising unsteadily to his foot. Father O'Brien had run across and was muttering over him. I thought he was administering the last rites but Jim Evans said he was remonstrating with him for scratching the polished dance floor with his iron leg.

"The three of us?" Surely Mrs Miley was not a practising troilist. But she was referring to her neutered bitch, Wilfred. "Certainly," I acquiesced. "I'll book the guest house tomorrow."

We left in time for our respective last buses. As we huddled in the shelter, I rubbed my hand over her right thigh on the pretext of looking for my pension pass. She didn't flinch but neither was she overcome by unbridled passion, merely offering to lend me 40p if I couldn't find it.

As her bus pulled in, I remembered the presents and searched in my

pockets for the Harods bag. Unfortunately, the Smarties and the flowers had suffered in my fall at the club and had united in a congealed mess. She accepted the chocolate coloured snowdrops gracefully.

Roll on next weekend.

MON FEB 4TH

I've had a terrible shock which has upset my whole system and put back the recovery of my nervous asthma by at least six months.

This morning, by first post, came a recorded delivery letter from a firm of solicitors in Clapham. It was a paternity suit. A 38 year old African social worker is accusing me of fathering her recent offspring, a boy called Jesus Basil. It is her eighth child but no mention has been made of any connection between myself and the previous seven.

I am perplexed. Try as I will, I am unable to recall a carnal encounter in recent months with a black woman 45 years my junior, an event that would not usually pass unnoticed, even in my action-packed life. Would that such episodes were a regular occurrence. Sadly, the truth is that since leaving Marge and Neville's for my little love-nest, the nearest I have come to unbridled passion was when I called round on Old Mrs Pemberton with her new bingo club card and caught a glimpse of her liberty bodice on her washing line. Not my idea of total fulfilment and hardly in the class of multi-racial couplings on Clapham Common, if indeed that is where the alleged incident took place.

The papers served on me give the date of conception as February 14th last year, suggesting I was delivering, perhaps, some sort of Valentine's Day treat. This puts me in a position to defend myself as I clearly recall I spent that day in the Casualty Department of the Clement Attlee Memorial Hospital after being attacked by a pack of rampant vegetarians. I had dared to cross their picket line outside a butcher's shop in Brixton where I was going to buy a brace of sheep's eyes.

But, on reflection, I realise I was not detained in the hospital, despite my cruel injuries, one of which required a stitch. So I suppose I could have gone on to commit this atrocity later, although whether I would have been in a fit state to do so is a matter of conjecture. I wouldn't mind but I am, myself, a macrobiotic vegetarian. I only wanted the sheep's eyes for little Begley's marble collection.

My diary for the evening of Valentine's Day last year is blank. I have listed the names of 14 women to whom I sent Valentines but the name of Bolvis Ngoomi is not amongst them.

I never knew a Bolvis Ngoomi. Sounds like a foreign brand of beef cube extract to me. How did she get hold of my name? Are there teams of travelling romeos wandering round Clapham, impregnating the local women then leaving my name as a calling card to protect them from dire consequences?

I obviously need an alibi.

The boil on my bottom is still festering. I fear it may become an abcess.

TUES FEB 5TH

Went to the doctor's for a note for my defence. "So soon, Mr Sherlock," snarled Dr Gavin. "Have the warts multiplied? Surely you've not finished the barrel of ointment? I said rub it on one day a week for 13 weeks not 13 times a day for one week. And how's the trouble with your bowels?"

"No better. I'd like some more of the white substance that Dr Patel gave me last year. I don't know what it was called."

"Probably heroin," he laughed. "Now is that all or did you come for something other than idle chatter?"

"Whatever happened to the bedside manner?"

"You're not in bed," he replied sanguinely. "You're dashing round the streets like an indefatigable Zeppelin left over from World War One."

I prodded his stethoscope. "I want a letter from you to say I am impotent, infertile and incapable."

"And are you?"

"I am after the shock I had yesterday." I told him about the letter.

"But it's only three months ago that you were in here asking for ginseng root to increase your potency. Did it help by the way?"

"Only if I used it as a splint. Look, I'm 84. I can't afford University fees on my pension."

"They've got to prove it first. Demand a blood test."

"I can't afford to give any blood. You still owe me a pint from last year when there was that shortage after the Aids scare."

"We're still short of your group. Would you like some cough medicine in lieu? You usually get your annual attack of croup around this time."

I ignored him. "I just want a note to say that I couldn't possibly have fathered a child in my condition."

"Have you no recollection of this person, the mother of your child?"

I winced at the thought. "None."

"Are you asking me, then, to claim amnesia on your behalf?"

"Couldn't you claim amputation? That'd get me off the hook."

"I'll perform the operation now, if you like. I've got a carving knife somewhere."

"Very funny. This isn't what we pay our National Health subscriptions for."

"As I see it, your only solution is to find out who gave this woman your name. It must be somebody who knows you." He chuckled. "It's the old story, Mr Sherlock. A grudge pregnancy. Someone had it in for you. Ha ha." He ushered me to the door and added coldly: "I am afraid I am not able to lie for you. Good morning."

I was on the street before I had time to mention the boil on my bottom.

WED FEB 6TH

The amazing truth has emerged. It was Neville who gave my name to Bolvis. Bolvis turns out to be Natalie's social worker, appointed to be responsible for her spiritual welfare after the trouble with the miners. They take the place of the clergy nowadays for five times the salary and with Sundays off.

Apparently, her idea of social work includes the provision of certain 'extra services' for sexually maladjusted white men of comfortable means which she offers at an establishment in the South London borough next to a second hand fruit shop.

For a once only instalment of £1,000, Neville is able to enjoy Bolvis's body between the hours of six and seven every Friday night on a Timeshare basis. Under the scheme, if he is unable to take up his occupancy during any of these periods, he can swop with another subscriber. Foreign exchanges are also catered for.

"She needed someone's name for the DHSS," he explained. "I gave yours because everyone knows that there's no way you could father a child at your age and in your condition."

How dare he! I have a good mind to admit to the deed. That would send my stock soaring at the Compton Road Social and Welfare Club.

And the DHSS would probably pay my court costs like they do everything else.

In the end, I agreed to take on Neville's next appointment and see what I have been missing. As long as my Queenie doesn't find out.

THURS FEB 7TH

My first day in my new job. I reported to a little office in Otis Redding Avenue where a team of us, none under 70, gathered to carry out a market research survey into feet.

A national shoe manufacturer wanted to compare the size of women's feet in different occupations. They wanted documentary evidence that policewomen really did have bigger feet than secretaries or part-time budgerigar breeders. It was all to do with the planning of their next advertising campaign.

Our job was to stop women in the street at random and ask them what size shoes they wore and what jobs they did. The hope was that some sort of pattern would emerge.

It was not easy work. Most women did not take kindly to being confronted by a senior citizen questioning them about the size of their appendages, even such innocent appendages as feet. Some of them misconstrued my approach.

"Bit old for kerb crawling aren't you?" sneered one lady. "Especially on foot. Can't you afford to go to a massage parlour?"

Others were reluctant to give away secret information. "How do I know you're not working for the Russians?" demanded a blue-rinsed Gorgon.

"Would the size of your feet interest Mr Gorbachev do you think?" I replied coldly. "Might the information advance his nuclear programme and embarrass the Americans?"

One strange girl with an orange Mohican haircut was delighted to be questioned but was not too certain about the size of her stiletto boots. "Hang on a minute, I've got a ruler here somewhere." She delved into a hessian rucksack, strewing various impedimenta, including her lunchtime ham sandwiches, onto the pavement.

Eventually, she found a plastic ruler that had seen better days. "I'll just take them off," she said, struggling with the calf length boots and finally descending to her bottom to obtain greater purchase.

By now, a small crowd of puzzled by-standers had gathered round to watch. I held my clipboard anxiously.

She removed her boots. "Here we go, left one first. I think it's a bit bigger than my right one."

"I bet it is, darlin'," smirked a passing youth in an Eddie Grundy accent.

A grimy toe quivered near my chin as she swivelled round. "How's that?"

"I think you've just sat on your sandwiches," I pointed out. The butter oozed out onto her jeans, merging with the miscellaneous stains. I reached down for the ruler only to find it measured only centimetres. "Haven't you got inches?" I asked. "I'm 84, I don't understand foreign currency."

She reached back in the rucksack but lost her balance and sprawled on the ground. At this point, a policeman arrived, attracted by the sideshow.

"Is this man bothering you, miss?"

"I'm just trying to measure her feet," I explained.

"Is this something you do regularly, sir?"

"Just on Thursdays at the moment," I stammered. "It's for market research. Trying to find out if policemen really do have bigger feet than . . ." I stopped in horror.

"Here's one." The girl handed me another ruler. "I think you'll find inches there; twelve of them."

I held it against her foot. The foot overlapped. "Would you mind putting your finger just there?" I asked the policeman, indicating a point close to the heel next to an oily pimple, "whilst I measure this last bit."

The policeman was not co-operative. "I'm giving you thirty seconds to move away from here or I'm taking you in for causing an obstruction." He bent down and threw the girl's boots onto her recumbent body. "And that goes for you, Genghis Khan."

A pigeon started to eat one of the ham sandwiches.

"But I haven't measured her feet yet," I protested.

He turned on me. "Look, Grandad. I don't know what game you're playing but you're a bit old for street theatre and probably haven't got a licence for it. You should be in your sheltered flat with a cup of Horlicks and the Sporting Life."

I bristled. "That's the second time today I've been told I'm too old. I'm younger than Mrs Thatcher and nobody tells her to go home and make a cup of Horlicks."

At this, several of the spectators shouted out suggestions for Mrs Thatcher to undertake, few of them physically possible. Things started to get boisterous. Someone tried to run off with the girl's boots. She leapt angrily to her (bare) feet, trod on the jagged edge of the plastic ruler and unfortunately knocked the policeman over.

More pigeons and the occasional starling now joined in the consumption of the ham sandwiches.

In the end, ten of us were taken to the Police Station and charged with causing an affray.

This is the end of my working career.

FRI FEB 8TH

The day of my encounter with Bolvis Ngoomi. I put on clean combinations for the occasion although I wasn't due for them until a week tomorrow.

Went into town this morning to buy an iron tonic to fortify me in readiness when, quite by chance, I bumped into Queenie who was queueing for her scrag end and weekly offal at the Market.

"I'm glad I ran into you, Walter," she said. "I'm afraid I have regretful tidings about our weekend outing at the seaside."

"But I've booked the room at the Bacchanalia Guest House."

"Did you use your own name?"

"No. I said we were Mr and Mrs Patel. After my doctor."

"That's all right then. They won't be able to trace you. Anyway, we can go next weekend. It's just that I've promised to look after my neighbours' tortoise tomorrow whilst they go to see his mother in Risley. But next week they'll look after Wilfred."

"Yes, well you can't put carnal ecstacy before the welfare of a dumb reptile," I agreed. Maybe it was as well. Two sudden bouts of strenuous activity in this direction after what seems like a lifetime of celibacy, might have been too much for my varicose veins.

"Why don't you take me to lunch instead?" she suggested. "McDonalds is just across the road."

Once inside, Queenie asked for a Big Mac. "I'm afraid you'll have to make do with a Little Mac," I said. "My money's tied up at the moment in unpaid War Credits."

"They only do Big Macs," she said. "I suppose we could cut one in half."

"With chips?" enquired the assistant.

"One portion," I said, quickly.

"And would you care for something to drink?"

"Tap water for me."

"Anything with it?"

"Just a cup."

We took our meal to a corner table. "I've always been blessed with thrifty men," sighed Queenie, as I counted our joint chips onto two paper plates. She held her plastic knife poised over the Big Mac. "Have you got a ruler, Walter, or should I make a wild guess?"

I took my portion and we munched on, the silence broken only by the clicking of Queenie's ill-fitting lower dentures.

"Would you care to accompany me on my afternoon outing?" she asked, as we finished our nourishing snack. "I was thinking of going along to the

Spiritualists. They're bolding an afternoon tea dance for old and new members—a sort of spiritual reunion."

I wrinkled my nose. "The music's always too loud at those do's. Enough to waken the dead."

"That's probably the intention," remarked Queenie. "After all, it is a reunion dance."

I was tempted to go but the thought of my meeting with Bolvis stopped me. "I'm afraid I have to see my son's social worker this afternoon. Another time perhaps. In fact, why don't you come with me on the Over 60's Summer Outing on Sunday? There's some seats left on the charabanc."

"It's February, Walter. Why would they be having a summer outing now?"

"It's to avoid the traffic jams. Besides, most of the Over 60's are abroad in the summer so they thought they'd move it forward this year."

"So long as there'll be time to feed the tortoise."

"Won't it be asleep this time of year?"

"Oh, I don't know. But I said I'd keep an eye on it."

"Well, if it looks asleep you can leave a bread roll outside its shell in case it wakes up."

"I suppose so."

"I'll book the seats then."

"Walter?" She looked at me shyly. "You've had a photograph of me. Do you think I could have one of you?"

I pulled open my wallet. "I've only got the one, Queenie." I handed her a torn sepia print.

"Oh, they're all soldiers. Were you in a War, Walter? Which regiment was it?"

"The West Lancashire Deserters. We met every year till 1939 to celebrate our escape."

"From the Germans?"

"From the Military Police. In 1939, we had to go into hiding again."

"I'll treasure it always, Walter. Er, which one are you?"

"The handsome one with the Rudolf Valentino eyes."

"Oh yes, and the Charlie Chaplin legs. Did you have rickets as a child?" She squinted at it closely. "Don't you look different with hair! And you've got most of your teeth here too."

"I *was* only 21." I pulled out my gold Hunter. "Gosh, is that the time? Until Sunday then, my sweet." I chanced a light kiss on her rouged, wrinkled cheek. She shivered joyfully.

"Until Sunday."

70

I quickly made my way to the Tube, stopping only at the Health Shop for a bottle of dandelion herb and iron tonic. I managed four mouthfuls on the journey and arrived at Clapham feeling slightly sick.

The establishment I was looking for was called the Clapham Massage Studio, according to the sign peeling off the window. Somebody had removed the 'ham' portion, suggesting the possibility of social disease lurking within its doors. The window itself was dressed with white drapes and a bowl of plastic flowers, not dissimilar to a Chapel of Rest. Perhaps some of the clients had found the activities too strenuous.

I walked inside. Only an oak desk adorned the shop and behind it sat a girl in a white coat reading a copy of 'The Plain Man's Guide to Haemorrhoids'.

"I'm Walter Sherlock," I said. "I have an assignation with Miss Ngoomi at six o'clock."

She looked up from her book with a surprised expression. "Are you all right, Mr Sherlock? You look different somehow."

"I've had a lot of problems in the past seven days," I explained. "I feel I've aged twenty years."

"Or even thirty," she agreed. "You've had some of your teeth out too, I see." Trust Neville to still keep all his own teeth at 50 when everyone else his age has a few decent gaps as a tribute to the virulence of the sugar industry.

"Well, you know what these dentists are like?" I smiled, trying to keep my mouth shut as much as possible. "Once they get going with those pliers, it's hard to stop them."

She leaned forward confidentially. "I'm afraid I have bad news for you. Miss Ngoomi is no longer with us."

"What!"

"She has been struck off our rota of masseurs." Her voice dropped to the hiss of an asthmatic puff adder. "She was offering extra services to selected clients."

"Really? What sort of extra services?"

"You know . . ." she giggled.

"You mean sandwiches, soft drinks, things like that?"

"No. I mean . . . sexual type services."

"Disgusting!"

"Quite. Gets the business a bad name. This is a reputable massage parlour. Our staff have degrees in Physiotherapy."

"Really," I said disappointedly.

"Anyway, nothing for you to worry about, Mr Sherlock." She consulted her work-sheet. "Six to seven aren't you. Yes, you've got Peter Coward. He used to be in the Marines. He'll give you a good going over. Now, do you want the baby oil massage?"

I shuddered. "No thank you. It will make my clean combinations sticky."

"The talc massage perhaps?"

"I'm allergic to dust."

She sighed. "Just the ordinary pounding then?"

"Er yes." I had never been keen on the Marines. "As a matter of fact, I think I might give it a miss this week. I've been having trouble with a rogue kidney and I wouldn't like to upset it. I'll see you next Friday. And book me Mr Coward again." That would serve Neville right.

Back to the flat alone. So much for my weekend of anticipated lechery. When I got in I found a puncture in my hot water bottle, the only thing I had left to cling to in bed.

SAT FEB 9TH

I decided to go to the dentist's after yesterday's remarks about my teeth. Found out that after 35 years in the practice, old Mr Barclay has retired and his place been taken by a Mr Sean Jewell, a Mr Nigel Prideham and a Mr Michael Bennett. Typical of your modern inflation.

I chose Mr Bennett as being the least Irish-sounding but had a big shock when, strapped to the chair by an enormous nurse, I was confronted by a lissom blonde.

"I'm not used to women interfering in my orifices," I complained. "I want Mr Bennett."

"I am Ms Bennett, Michaela Bennett, they missed the 'a' out in the sign. And as for your orifices, it's about time someone looked into this one. It's like a foetid cavern in there. When did you last have dental treatment?"

"Last year but Old Mr Barclay's eyesight wasn't at its best in later years."

"Neither was his sense of smell if he didn't notice something was amiss in that stinking hellhole."

"You have an astute grasp of medical terms," I said. "What are you going to do about my treatment?"

"What do you want me to do?"

"I'd like all my bottom teeth out."

"All? There's only one."

"Quite. And I've had enough of it. It keeps moving about. Just as I get my mouth nicely positioned to bite my chocolate finger, the bugger moves to one side and I miss it."

"How awful. At least it keeps your consumption of biscuits down." She wiggled it from side to side with her fingers. "I'll have that out in no time. Hang on, though, there's another one down here."

"I think you're mistaken. I've only had the one for years."

"No I'm not. It's definitely got a little friend, albeit a covered stump. I'll be able to dig down and get it though."

I flinched. She made it sound like an archaeological expedition. "The top ones are all my own," I assured her.

"So I observe. Such a charming array of autumn colours they present. Tell me, have you had your halitosis for long?"

"I beg your pardon."

"I suppose you've smoked a lot." She took a needle from a tray and filled it with a pink liquid. "I'll give you an injection to deaden the pain."

I could have done with an injection to deaden the injection. But it was better than gas. There is always the chance the dentist will interfere with you during unconsciousness although, in Ms Bennett's case, that might have been a bonus.

The tooth was extracted with no more than the average excruciating agony. The stump followed. "Right," said Ms Bennett. "Let's discuss your new dentures."

"I'd like pointed ones. Better for chewing."

"You'd look like Dracula. Why not some even white ones?" She handed me a catalogue. "Have a look at some of these."

I flicked through the pages. "A bit old isn't it? Half the pictures are faded. How about these—the Douglas Fairbanks Jnr set?"

"35 years out of date," she said, "but probably in keeping with your image. Our only problem now is what to do with those hideous things quietly rotting in your top gums like a row of vandalised gravestones. They'll have to go."

"Why? They work all right."

"They won't match your new bottom set."

"Get me some brown ones at the bottom, then. I'm 84. I can't have 20-odd teeth out at my age. I'd never survive the operation." At this point, she leaned over the spitoon and I caught a glimpse of red suspenders. "Perhaps I could have one out every week until they were all gone. I think my constitution could stand that."

We settled for six a month. Meanwhile, she is ordering the Douglas Fairbanks and I go next week for the impression.

Queenie won't know me.

SUN FEB 10TH

Denuded of my bottom tooth, or teeth as it turned out, I had to suck my cornflakes at breakfast and dip my toast and marmalade in my tea.

Met Mrs Miley at the Over 60's at ten, just in time for the arrival of the charabanc. I pushed her forward into the surging throng of pensioners, all flailing about with their walking sticks, trying to get to the window seats.

Thanks to a judicious nudge which landed Old Mrs Pemberton head first against the accelerator pedal, I was able to steer Queenie into the back seat where we were joined by Jim Evans and his wife.

Jim leered across at me from his corner and waved a clenched fist suggestively. "I know why you want the back seat, Walter."

"What does he mean?" asked Queenie.

"I've no idea. I sit here because I don't like being over the wheel."

"Shouldn't we ladies be sitting beside the window?" Queenie ventured demurely.

Jim Evans was quick to shake his head. "We'd never forgive ourselves if there was an accident and you were disfigured for life by flying glass."

"But it's toughened glass they use nowadays."

"Precisely. Cuts you even worse than the ordinary sort."

Mrs Evans said nothing. She looked hollow cheeked so I presumed that Jim had bagged the family dentures for the day; unless, of course, they were swopping over at lunchtime.

We had not been on the road five minutes when a buzzer sounded and Scabby Walmsley staggered to the front of the bus. The driver pulled up and Scabby tottered out and dashed behind a convenient hedge.

"That's his alarm to say his bag's full," explained his travelling companion and supposed mistress, Mrs Francis.

"Couldn't he have checked it before he came out?" complained someone. "We all made sure we went before we set off."

"I didn't," remarked Jim Evans, "but you've put the idea in my head." He lumbered down the aisle and off the coach.

"Wait for me," cried Lionel Lang, "it was all that coffee I had at breakfast."

Within a minute, there were half a dozen of them relieving themselves behind the hedge.

"I wouldn't mind," said Mrs Miley, distastefully, "but that is someone's garden. It's a good job they seem to be out."

"It'll bring on their tulips early, anyway," I said. "They'll have cause to be grateful in the long run."

The rest of the journey continued uneventfully. Several times I allowed my arm to brush against Queenie's bosom which overlapped round the edge of her Methodist Recorder like a creeping bolster. She read on relentlessly.

As most of our party suffered from advanced decay of their bowel systems, we made frequent stops en route and it was lunch time before we reached the sea.

Our meal was booked at The Palm Court which sounded rather grand but which turned out to be a glorified fish and chip shop which smelt of rancid fat and drying raincoats. Luckily, I had come prepared for such an eventuality and took out a Harvest Crunch biscuit.

The proprietor, however, was obviously no exponent of healthy eating. He pointed to a notice forbidding the consumption of one's own food on the premises and suggested that I retire to the bus shelter outside if I did not wish to partake of his recently defrosted haddock.

It was damp and cold in the bus shelter. I thought Queenie might have made a stand and walked out with me in protest but she remained steadfast in her seat, munching her rancid chips with a hearty vigour.

In the afternoon, we were led to the deserted fairground where everyone made a beeline for the Bingo Parlour.

"Let's go in The River Caves," I suggested to Queenie.

"In this weather? It'll be freezing."

"They can hardly have central heating in The River Caves," I pointed out. "The Big Wheel then."

"No thank you. I get vertigo in the Hall of Mirrors. Besides, everything's shut for the winter. February's not a big month for fairgrounds. Let's get in the Bingo Parlour before my rheumatism starts up."

Reluctantly, I took my place at the tables. This was obviously the only place of entertainment open in the town because it was packed out.

"Good job we came when we did," remarked Queenie, "or we'd never have got a game. I've never seen so many people."

"The world's overcrowded," I said glumly. "This, of course, is why the Government has brought in this Aids, in order to get the numbers down a bit."

On the fifth game, Queenie squealed like a startled ferret. "Line! Line! Oooh, Walter, I've won, I've won. I wonder what I'll get?"

"I shouldn't get too worked up," I said. "Lionel Lang won a full house and all he got was a faded tea towel commemorating the Pope's visit to Kampala in 1969."

Queenie got a mug, inscribed with a picture of Princess Margaret on one side and Lord Snowdon on the other. "Have they remarried then?" she asked.

"1960 they married. Probably they'd run out of the Coronation mugs."

"It'll do to put my teeth in at night," said Queenie. "I'm always worried about getting them broken, rattling round in the sink."

"We've got other prizes, lady," said the bingo caller, noticing Queenie's lack of immediate joy at her prize. "You can have a black and white poster of The Inkspots or how about a pair of luminous nail clippers for your old Dad there?"

"How dare you!" I cried. "That's it. I've had enough. I'm going back to the chara." And I stormed out into the force nine gale.

"What about your tea?" Queenie screeched after me.

"If it's anything like the lunch, they can stick it."

Three hours later, reunited in the coach, we set off for home. "Pity you didn't come for tea, Walter," said Queenie. "The vegetable casserole was lovely. I hope you weren't too cold in that shelter. Shame the coach was locked up."

I said nothing but, as we reached the open road, I placed my coat over our knees and slid my hand towards Queenie until our fingers were touching. I took hold of them and squeezed. "Do you mind!" shouted Jim Evans and snatched his hand away.

"My mistake," I muttered. It had seemed rather hairy. I wondered what Jim Evans' hand had been doing on Queenie's knee. A few minutes later, I tried again.

"How dare you!" snapped Queenie to Jim Evans and took my coat away. The rest of the journey passed in silence. I counted street lamps, Queenie resumed her study of the Methodist Recorder and Jim Evans fell asleep. So much for a fun day out. Next weekend had better be better.

MON FEB 11TH

High excitement at this afternoon's Senior Citizens Meeting at the Assembly of God's Chosen Brethren Mission Hall. A new member joined—a widowed lady with a blue rinse and an artificial hip called Mrs Chisholm. Her late husband made his pile in the War masterminding an undercover pork pie factory in Golders Green. When hostilities ceased, they retired to Chipping Norton but the rarified mountain air of the Cotswolds did not agree with him and he fell victim to cirrhosis of the liver, a condition that was very fashionable in Mr Macmillan's Days of Plenty.

Obviously his wife had benefited financially from his sad demise as she was festooned with rings and furs from badly protected animals. I found it pathetic to see how the men fawned over her. When she took out a cigarette, lighters were thrust at her from all sides, and even when she disdainfully produced her own box of matches Jacob Dickins was there offering his steel-toed artificial leg for her to strike one on.

"Would you care for a glass of Bovril, madam?" I enquired solicitously in a lull between the week's Members' Obituaries and the Housey Housey.

"Thank you, no. You're the seventh person that has offered but, as I told the other six, I am quite happy with my lukewarm coffee and bloater paste sandwiches."

"Yes, quite," I said. "The Assembly of God's Chosen Brethren have always been noted for their upmarket catering. Er, if you should be concerned about walking home with the poor street lighting and cracked pavements that are the legacy of a Labour council, I would be happy to walk you home."

She put down her cup of coffee. "Thank you but I have my Rover outside."

"Tied up to the railings, is he?" I said. "Such good companions dogs."

"My Rover 700," she said frostily. "Not a vehicle to concern itself with cracked pavements and equipped, thankfully, with powerful headlamps that negate the mediocrity of the street lighting."

So much for my chances of luring her into a warm shop doorway. I still have fond memories of an encounter in the Derbyshire Building Society doorway in Nebuchadnezzar Street in 1942 with Mrs Nyman who had, it was said, accommodated most of the Panzer Division of the American Army as part of her War Effort.

What with the celibate nature of my romantic liaison with Queenie, I fear I am losing my touch with women. Are my days in shop doorways numbered? Am I doomed to spending my declining years in my expensively rented love nest with only my poster of Mrs Thatcher for company?

Having run out of Tuinal, I took an extra teaspoon of Horlicks in my milk before retiring to help blot out the memory of the day. Doesn't have as speedy an effect though. Wish Natalie had left some of her funny cigarettes behind.

TUES FEB 12TH

I decided to start the day by doing myself in. Left a note on the toaster, explaining to Marge and Neville that the continuing poor form of Everton Reserves had driven me to the end of my tether.

I ate a hearty breakfast, there being no reason to deprive the pathologist

77

of the pleasure of sifting through a full stomach at my post mortem. Also, it would have been wasteful to leave behind half a packet of Shreddies.

Dressed in my new bowler and demob suit, I set out for Denis Compton House, the tallest building in town which housed the council offices.

"Fourteenth floor," I instructed the lift attendant.

"You'll have a job, Grandad. We only go up to six."

"Sixth floor then."

"What do you want exactly?"

"What's on the sixth floor?"

"Pregnancy counselling."

"Yes, that's it."

He looked at me strangely. "Bit old for that ain't yer?"

"It's not for me," I persisted. "It's for my wife."

"'ere," he said. "You're another jumper ain't yer?"

"I don't know what you mean."

"We get two or three a week in 'ere, jumpers. Highest building in town, see? Under Mrs Thatcher's caring government, we find there's a big demand among the old and destitute to see what the alternative has to offer."

"You mean Mr Kinnock?"

"I mean The Other Side," he whispered. "The Great Divide." He leant closer to my face. "Jack, the caretaker, has a special shovel he uses for scraping them off the pavement. They always seem to splatter down just by his cokehouse door." He went back to the lift lever. "Sixth floor did you say?"

"Er, maybe I'll settle for the fourth."

"Don't give the buggers the satisfaction of beating yer," he advised. "Why don't you go and see The Samaritans?"

"Do you think they'll help people in mental torment?"

"No. But you'll get a free cup of tea and a chocolate biscuit out of them and it's a change from going to the pictures every afternoon."

There goes a man, I thought, who understands the lifestyle of a senior citizen. I went straight round to The Samaritans office, a tumbledown shop between the Launderama and a barber's shop selling slightly used hairpieces and unusual marital devices.

"Can I help you?" enquired the assistant, a girl of about 23 with white make-up and green streaked hair.

"I shouldn't imagine so," I replied. "I came to see a Samaritan not a talking lampshade."

"I am a Samaritan," she said. "What is it you want?"

"Well, I was going to kill myself but I'm told you have to come here first."

"That's right," she said. "Sit down will you and I'll get you a cup of tea. Then you can tell me about your problems."

"Don't forget the chocolate biscuits," I shouted but she had already disappeared into the back room. I looked around the shop. On the plastered walls were posters depicting the fate of heroin addicts, warnings against the evils of smoking, drinking and promiscuous sex, plus advice on treating hidden social diseases in secret. Nothing there, I felt, to make you feel life was worth living.

"Why don't you have pictures of the countryside or menus from the best hotels?" I asked, when she reappeared with the tea. "Something to encourage us to change our minds."

"By the look of you," she said, "I think you're making the right choice. You can't have much to look forward to when you get to such a great age. Have a Jaffa cake."

"I'm only 84," I protested. "I could give you a good time."

"It'll cost you," she said. "What's your problem, anyway? Why do you want to top yourself?"

"I've not made up my mind for certain," I said defiantly. "I was only considering it. I came in here hoping you'd give me a good reason to dissuade me."

"Couldn't do that," she said. "You'd never forgive me if you lived to regret it, so to speak. Whereupon, if you go ahead and do it then you won't be around to regret anything and there'll be no comeback on me, see."

"But I'm concerned I'm losing my grip on things."

"Is there nobody to look after you?"

"My parents are dead," I admitted sadly. "The rest of my family emigrated to Grimsby in the 1958 Herring Rush."

"Have you never had a wife?"

"I've had five but they all escaped."

She consulted a handbook. "Pity you're not black, I could have got you a social worker."

"Can't I have one if I'm white?"

"Only if you're a criminal or a disabled Lesbian with militant tendencies."

"I do have a walking stick."

"A white one?"

"Surely there's no discrimination against walking sticks."

"A white one would mean you were blind," she said patiently. "Would you like to go into a home?"

"Yours?"

79

"I was thinking more of the Mussolini Institution for Poor Retired Gentlefolk in Delhi Street. You'd have lots of company and the fees aren't expensive."

"No need to worry about the fees," I assured her. "I have a personal benefactor."

"The DHSS you mean? I'm with them too. This is only voluntary work here, you know. I don't HAVE to come here. I could be out enjoying myself now but someone has to look after poor buggers like you."

"Very noble of you."

"Yes, they're very good the DHSS. We send each other customers. Backwards and forwards they go from our office to theirs, never knowing whether they're coming into a windfall from the State or heading for the top floor of a large building to end it all and claim the death grant."

"That's what I was going to do," I said. "Jump off the sixth floor of the Denis Compton House. And I feel so miserable now I think I might go back."

"Don't do that," she said quickly. "You'd be better off on the second floor of the Port Buildings by the river. Less stairs to walk up and water isn't so hard when you hit it. And with a good tide, you'll drown in no time."

"I shouldn't give you the satisfaction," I snarled and marched out of the shop. Obviously she is on commission from the Crematorium. Is there nothing nowadays people will not do for backhanders?

Rushed home to find my suicide note to Marge and Neville had fallen into the toaster and burned. So they would never have known why I'd done it.

WED FEB 13TH

Much brighter start to the day. My list of available women arrived from the Computer Dating Agency. Convinced myself that, as I had not had carnal knowledge of Queenie's person, I was not being unfaithful to her.

However, on closer examination of the list of names, I found only one of the six suitable.

After the unfortunate episode with Bolvis Ngoomi, plus the fact that I had specifically ordered Caucasian women, it came as a great disappointment to see the first two names on the list were Ho Kay Ching and Minerva Sawamatsu.

Of course, they could have been widows from the Colonies, born and bred in Stow-in-the-Wold, but I was not inclined to take a chance.

No. 3 on the list sounded better—Jillian Collins. Perhaps a cousin of

Joan. As she lived in Aberdeen, however, 760 miles outside the boundary of my bus pass, it was unlikely I would ever find out.

Remembering my firm rejection of the religious boxes on the application form, I was surprised to see the name of Sister Maria-Theresa on the list. Obviously this was her escape route from the open convent in the Mendips where she presently resided.

I could only conclude that the next name was a typist's error. Not only did Horatio Wellington Arthur sound suspiciously black, he also sounded like he might possibly be a man. This was a great worry. Could my own name be on a list circulating amongst Horatio's jolly companions? If so, my reputation in the house could be ruined if a bunch of arpees started ringing up and Mr Murray answered the phone.

Even worse; Ron Alley might answer the phone and become re-converted and Mrs Newfoundland would lose him forever.

All of which left me with just one name, that of Enid O'Leary from County Down. She was 46 and divorced. Unlikely to be a virgin then, as requested, and probably a gun-runner for the IRA. There was always the chance that her husband had been in the Maze prison since their nuptials, and the marriage might yet be annulled, but it was not a likely possibility.

Obviously they are scraping the bottom of the barrel at the Computer Dating Agency. Or are there really no white vegetarians left in England who are not raving nymphomaniacs?

I decided to write to this woman but, to be on the safe side, enclosed a photo of Jacob Dickins taken when he was invalided out of the trenches in 1918. How I shall explain the acquisition of an extra leg I shall decide later.

THURS FEB 14TH

Valentine's Day. I sent seven cards only this year. To Queenie, a large Romantic one bearing the inscription 'mine until the end of time' from the Market with a yellow envelope for only 35p. I signed it 'from a secret admirer with love from Walter'.

As a safeguard for the future, I posted humorous greetings to Mrs Hylands, Mrs Jessup, Mrs Washington, Old Mrs Pemberton, and Mrs O'Leary in County Down in anticipation of her visit.

Although I have dismissed Mrs Washington as a septugenarian whore, one must not be pedantic about these things. One day, I might be desperate.

Similarly with Old Mrs Pemberton. Her classes in Advanced Cosmetics have done nothing to alleviate the deep ridges in her skin which look like

81

they have been filled in with something from the builders' yard rather than The Body Shop. Old Mrs Pemberton has dedicated most of her ninety years to the maintenance of her face but, sad to say, it has all been a waste of time.

As there were six cards in the special offer pack, I sent the last one to Jim Evans, signed 'love and passion from Lily' which should speed up divorce proceedings if Mrs Evans claps her eyes on it.

All six cards carried the words 'to the only one I love' written across the naked buttocks of a twenty three stone woman.

I, myself, received just the one card. It was unsigned but I recognised Queenie's joined-up writing on the envelope. Pencilled on the back was 1/3d!

My other letter brought the welcome tidings that the police have decided not to prosecute me over the street affray last week.

Encouraged by this news, I spent the rest of the day filling in competition forms in the papers.

I have never had much luck in competitions since I was eight and was refused a winning night out with Clara Bow because I was under age. I never got over the disappointment. I might not have been able to offer her much in the way of sparkling conversation but I could have given her a great time on the helter skelter with ice cream and chips to follow.

I suppose, at 84, I have really reached the stage of life where, even if I were to win, the prizes would be of little use to me. The opportunity to train with the Everton football team courtesy of the Sporting Life might aggravate my chronic rheumatism not to mention play havoc with my ingrowing toe nail.

Similarly, the chance of a guest role in 'Dallas', possibly a brief marriage to Sue Ellen, would be impractical on health grounds. Those vicious winds that lash the patio at Southfork could easily herald a return of the galloping consumption that has run in the family since 1660. Besides, I don't have a pair of shoulder pads that still fit me.

Perhaps, as a young man, I might have welcomed the Catholic Herald star prize but it is a bit late now for a free vasectomy. On the other hand, it does sound more exciting than the second prize—a night out with the Pope.

Many of the prizes aren't worth winning. Who wants a year's supply of soft toilet paper? Where would one put it all? Friends calling for dinner would assume you had a rare tropical disease and make their excuses, or accuse you of stockpiling in anticipation of a future Labour government, thus displaying greed and parsimony of the worst kind.

Several competitions offer holidays abroad. I have never fancied Afghanistan, even before the fighting. Luckily, I read the small print. You might fly out by Concorde but the return journey is across the desert in a Suzuki Rhino. All they are doing is giving away holidays they can't sell. Who wants to go on the Trans-Siberian Railway in January?

I once completed the Daily Telegraph Prize Crossword but was cheated out of the prize by a strike of militant postal sorters in Lambeth. My entry arrived two months late.

In the end, I decided to enter a competition with a slogan. I've always been good with slogans. 'Pedigree Chum makes your coat sparkle. And your dog will love it too'.

This one was for washing powder. I tried the trusted method of slagging off the opposition and wrote 'all other powders make your combinations itchy and give you chapped legs'.

If I win I get a night out with Michael Crawford courtesy of Woman's Realm. I wonder if I will be quite what Michael Crawford is expecting.

To bed early as tomorrow I have to be at the TV studios at seven. This film company were advertising for locals to be extras and Jim Evans put my name down. He said it could be the start of a new career for me as a Media Attraction.

I suppose it will be better than measuring feet.

FRI FEB 15TH

So much for my ambition to become the mature Cary Grant.

Spent a horrendous day filming. I wish I'd never become an extra now. It's all Jim Evans' fault. He assured me that, due to the chronic shortage of actors over 80 (caused by the popularity of sudden demise amongst 70 year old actors), early stardom would soon be thrust upon me.

"Apart from Max Wall," he said, "who do you know that's older than you and appears regularly on television?"

"Lots," I replied. "There's Lilian Gish, Charlie Chaplin, Mae West . . ."

"I think you'll find they're deceased," retorted Jim Evans icily. "This is your trump card. You are still a living actor which could give you the edge in the Casting Department."

I haven't got much faith in the Casting Department. When I presented myself at the studio in the early hours of the morning, I was informed that I would be playing a soldier in Northern Ireland.

"At 84?" I exclaimed. "Do they take them that old over there?"

"Everyone's a soldier in Northern Ireland, Grandad."

"Will I get to speak?"

"Only if you get hit by a brick, in which case you may cry out briefly in anguish." Note the 'briefly'. If you cry out more than five words, they have to pay you extra. A fellow called Jack Heathcoat was once hit over the head with an iron bar in a mock bank raid and managed to stagger halfway down the road screaming 'Oh God, the awful agony, when will it end?' when, in real life, he would have been in serious need of a life support machine. He was fired.

"Brick," I said quickly. "Why should I get hit by a brick?"

"Because you're in the Belfast riots. You're fleeing from rampaging Catholics who are burning your street down." Or maybe he said rampaging Protestants. Either way, whatever their spiritual persuasion, they were definitely running amok. And with bricks.

"Being careful," he added, "to avoid the Loyalist militia, who'll be attacking from their armoured cars, and the flames from the houses which we shall actually be setting on fire when we start shooting."

Our next stop was Wardrobe where we were issued with shirts and flannels.

"Hang on," I protested. "It's freezing outside, you know. This is the middle of January."

"Not in the plot it isn't. It's the middle of August."

At 7.30 a.m. a convoy of coaches took us all to a street of terraced houses which were awaiting demolition. Altogether there were 250 extras, all of them men.

"I only took this job to meet young starlets," I said to my travelling companion on the coach, a black-haired man with an unpleasant skin condition.

"You weren't on 'Last Battle' by any chance?" he asked. "Only, three blokes about your age DIED on that. Ninety-odd they were."

"I'm only 84," I pointed out.

"Hypothermia. They had to crawl around this field in Millom at three in the morning wearing only horsehair nightshirts and wintergreen, pretending to be peasants in the French Revolution. Someone told me that they hung on to them for a couple of days and used them as corpses in the next scene."

"Extra money for their widows, I suppose," I said gloomily, glad I had managed to retain my thermal underwear.

The ASM came down the aisle with a clipboard. "Are you Catholic or Protestant?" he enquired.

"You ask me that already?" blinked my companion whose name turned out to be Cohen.

The ASM groaned. "Christ, that's all we need, a bleedin' Irish Jew."

"Did someone say Irish Stew?" shouted one of the Protestants. "About time too. We've not had any breakfast yet."

Before the ASM could reply, the coach lurched to a halt beside a burnt-out double decker bus and two shells of motor cars.

"Right! Out of the coach and huddle against the far wall till we call you."

Dawn was just breaking as we clambered out into the freezing morning air. Hardly had we all disembarked before the coach driver set off again, obviously hoping to avoid the same fate as the double decker bus. We were marooned.

"When are you going to set fire to the houses?" I asked, thinking the flames might raise the temperature slightly.

"Hang on, lads. Here comes the rain." Big drops started to fall but there was no shelter, the houses being boarded up. The wind whipped down the narrow street, lashing the rain against our barely protected bodies. Someone asked about umbrellas but was told they would only blow inside out.

I reminded the director about The Chill Factor, the effect of a cold wind on wet clothes on ageing humans, but he was unmoved.

"You're the one that wants to be a film star."

"When are we getting a warm drink?" enquired another elderly chappie. I noticed that, contrary to Jim Evans' observations, there appeared to be many extras in the over 80 bracket although, if the weather stayed like this all day, few could be expected to survive to the next production. "Only I've been up since 5 o'clock."

"You'll get it when we're bloody ready," barked the ASM who had had the benefit of a public school education.

"Excuse me." A frail, white-haired pensioner shuffled forward, his ribs showing through the soaked open-necked shirt. "I've lost all the feeling in my member."

The ASM looked unconcerned. "Not to worry. You won't be needing it in this film and there's not much chance of you being offered 'Emmanuelle'."

"But it might be frostbite, it might drop off." He looked anxious. "In fact, it might have dropped off already." Everyone moved forward to search for the missing organ among the cobbles.

"For God's sake," roared the director. "Look, once you start rioting, you'll be warm enough." He pulled his oilskin over his fur-lined anorak.

"Now, I want all the Protestants at the other end of the street and when the Micks come out of their burning houses, let them have it with the bricks. Have you got that, Moses?"

Mr Cohen nodded sadly. "It's not as if I need the money," he whispered to me. "I've got a prosperous bagle business in Golders Green. And I need this?"

"Right. Now, as soon as we get the boards down, all you Catholics get inside the houses. As soon as you're inside, we'll set fire to them whereupon you all come out screaming and race up the street where the tanks will try to mow you down. This is when you pick up the sponge bricks and hurl them at the tanks."

The ASM coughed. "Er, I'm afraid we've run out of sponge bricks, Evelyn."

The director was nonplussed. "That's all right. We'll have to use the real ones then. Just remember to duck when the Protestants throw them back at you."

The houses were unboarded and we Catholics raced for the shelter they afforded. Seven men were injured in the crush to get out of the rain and were taken to hospital to have their bones set.

"And the bloody riot hasn't even started yet," grumbled the director who, in a previous generation, would have been one of the organisers of World War One.

At a given signal, the houses were fired and, as the flames roared around us, we ran out into the street into the path of the rampaging Protestants who had jumped the gun and arrived thirty seconds early. Something called the domino effect came into play and we all ended up in a tangled heap on the wet cobbles.

"Here, I think I've found that fella's whatsit," cried a youth, holding up what, on closer inspection, turned out to be a partially cooked sausage from the mobile canteen.

"Auction it," suggested someone. "You could make a few bob."

I noticed that I, too, had lost all feeling in MY personal regions and put it down to the lack of buttons on my pre-1950 flies which allowed the freezing wind a free passage in that direction.

"Right. Back to your places for another rehearsal."

"But the houses are blazing, we can't go in there."

"We're going for realism," said the director. "We'll make it a take before someone gets fried."

After three takes amidst the impressive conflagration, breakfast was called. The fat owner of the butty wagon seemed uninterested in my

vegetarian requirements and handed me a wedge of white bread stuffed with greasy bacon, an underdone sausage, which I examined twice to be sure, and a piece of black pudding resembling the stool of a constipated rabbit. "Tea or coffee?" he asked, pointing to twin verdigrised urns.

"Have you no Perrier water?" I asked. He looked at me and walked away. Meanwhile, there were rumblings of discontent among the extras.

"I've had enough," moaned one of them. "I'd be off now except they've got my trousers."

"Don't let that stop you," said his mate. "They're better than the pair you had on. I'm off when I've finished my grub."

"Won't they miss you?" I enquired.

"In all that lot? I shouldn't think so. Besides, I don't know if you noticed, but half the blokes who live in the next street joined in last time. There must have been over 300 of them battling it out there. If we stay, there won't be enough dinners to go round. We'd be doing the buggers a favour. They've got our names, we'll get the money, so let's scarper that's what I say."

It was a convincing argument.

"You're a Mick, ain't yer?" he said. I confessed I was. "You should've seen all you lot when you ran out of them burning houses. With the heat on your wet clothes, you was all steaming like a collection of electric kettles on legs."

He put his plate down. "Right, I'm off. Who's coming?" The response was bigger than I anticipated. At least fifty extras galloped round the corner and legged it until they came to a main road with a bus route.

I was at Marge and Neville's by lunch time where I was put in a hot bath and then wrapped in poultices. "Enough to give you triple pneumonia," scolded Marge. "There'll be no more of this acting business at your age. Why can't you retire gracefully into one of Lord Snowdon's automatic wheelchairs like other men do?"

I just hope the feeling returns to my personal regions before my 'honeymoon' tomorrow night with Queenie. The room at the Bacchanalia Guest House is booked. I look forward to a night of licentious pleasure.

SAT FEB 16TH

At last! The big day! My weekend with Queenie. Jim Evans called round first thing with a word of caution. "I take it you're well prepared for this event, Walter."

"Queenie's 76, Jim. I don't think there's much chance of getting her into trouble now."

"What I meant was, I hope you don't get let down at a vital moment so to speak. What you need, Walter, is a Blakoe Energiser. Makes a man more outstanding where it matters."

"In his wallet, you mean?"

He ignored me. "It's all to do with the circulation of the blood. The way I understand it, it builds up a little reservoir ready to pump the blood into action when you are ready for it."

"Thank you very much but I prefer to let my blood ooze through my veins like sludge the way it always has."

Queenie was waiting for me at the station spot on nine. Always a romantic, I handed her some chocolates as I greeted her.

"How kind, Walter, my favourites," she said. "Cadbury's Buttons. Are we in time for the train?" She handed me a gargantuan suitcase and I was glad I was wearing my best truss with the double elastic.

"Plenty of time," I said. "Should I get you a magazine for the journey?"

"Yes, and I'll go to the Ladies."

"I'm afraid they hadn't got the Woman's Weekly," I said when she returned, "so I got you the Practical Poultry Keeper. I hope that'll be all right."

"As long as it has recipes," she replied. "I'd have perhaps liked something a little more exciting though. Was there nothing with Mad Dan Quigley in?"

"Who's he? An all-in wrestler?"

"No, a mass murderer. He's in Broadmoor. They're always doing features on him in Real Life Detective. Is everything OK at the guest house, by the way?"

"Yes, except I had to change the names when I booked again. We're Mr and Mrs Molotov now. I used a different voice after last time."

Queenie looked worried. "I hope I won't have to speak in Russian. Only I might get the wrong breakfast."

When we were on the train. I made my first tentative move of affection. I slid my hand along her left thigh. "Not so early in the morning, Walter," she said. "It can make you bilious." Then she squeezed my hand. "Plenty of time tonight."

The journey, via various changes of train and bus, took three hours by which time, after carting Queenie's suitcase, I was beginning to wish I'd availed myself of Jim Evans' appliance.

"You're on the fourth floor," the landlady informed us. "The stairs are at the end of the passage."

We entered the bedroom, scene of our planned love nest, in a state of collapse. "Cold, isn't it," gasped Queenie. "Lucky I brought my bedsocks."

I fought for my breath and tried to remember where I'd seen the advert for a second hand pacemaker going cheap. ('Owner no longer has any use for it'!)

"Are you all right, Walter? Only you've gone the colour of curdled Complan."

I managed to open my mouth a couple of times like a whistling goldfish but no sound came out. Queenie set about unpacking her case, pulling out layer after layer of clothes.

"We've only come for the weekend," I managed to say, "not the winter."

"I'll need these, Walter. It's freezing although I see you're sweating somewhat."

"I can find ways of warming you up," I leered and lurched to my feet with arms outstretched. She pushed me back on the bed. "Not on an empty stomach. Let's go and have some lunch instead."

Back we trekked down the stairs, stopping at Reception to enquire about restaurants. "Can you recommend a good Vegetarian one?" I asked in the clipped tones of an East European émigré.

"I'm sorry, Mr Molotov. My husband and I are ardent carnivores."

We settled for toasted teacake and a slice of processed cheese at the Ronald Reagan Tearooms. "I thought we might go to the pictures this afternoon," suggested Queenie. "Have you seen 'Doctor on the Job'?"

I choked on my penultimate currant. Memories of Mrs Hyland came floating back to me. "Er, a medical film is it?"

"No, a comedy. It's a bit saucy but you won't mind that will you, Walter?" She touched my ankle with her fur-lined boot under the table and smiled invitingly.

But there was bad news at the cinema. "I'm afraid 'Doctor on the Job' finished yesterday," said the cashier. "It's '101 Dalmatians' today."

"Are there no other cinemas in town?" I demanded, angrily.

"Sorry, dear. Only a bingo parlour and a ten pin bowling alley."

"We'll go bowling," I said to Queenie. "I've never tried that."

"Let's go tomorrow," she said. "I'd like to see '101 Dalmatians' again."

"Can we have the back row?" I asked the cashier.

"You can have anywhere you like, love," she replied. "You're the only ones in."

"I'll have a Vanilla Surprise to take in with me," said Queenie. "With chocolate sauce and a milk flake."

90

I paid up dutifully, used to a life of pandering to the expensive whims of extravagant women. We took our places on the back row and I slid my arm round Queenie's shoulders. "Alone at last," I murmured in my Humphrey Bogart growl.

"Have you got a sore throat, Walter?" She opened her handbag. "I think I've got a lozenge saved in my hanky."

I waved her hand away and silently stroked her arm. She giggled girlishly. Tentatively, I moved my lips to hers but, unfortunately, this move coincided with the transportation of the ice cream to her lips and I ended up with Vanilla Surprise on my nose.

"Plenty of time for that tonight," Queenie said. "Let's sit back and enjoy the doggies shall we?"

The film lasted 96 minutes but it seemed like a week. I restricted my advances to the occasional squeeze of Queenie's hand, having taken 54 minutes to extract my arm from round her shoulders in a state of agonising cramp.

After the cinema, we returned to the Ronald Reagan Tearooms for dry egg and cress sandwiches and individual cream puffs before making our way back to the guest house.

"What time do you like to retire, Walter?" Queenie asked.

"Not too early," I replied. "I like to wait up for the end of The Archers."

"Twenty past seven's a bit early isn't it? They might think we're on our honeymoon and wink at each other in the corridors. I think we should show our faces in the television lounge."

The television lounge was a sombre room painted in dark brown with low red lighting and a one bar electric fire, conditions ideally suited to growing mushrooms. The picture on the 12" mahogany set was black and white.

"To think," I said, "when that television was made, we still had an Empire."

At ten o'clock, I enquired about the possibility of evening cocoa. "No room service after nine I'm afraid, but the bar is open. Perhaps you'd care for a cocktail, Mr Molotov?"

I shook my head. "No. I don't want to introduce Mrs Molotov to strong drink. It might affect her performance. Thank you all the same."

I collected Queenie and we climbed the four flights to our room. "These stairs have given me an awful headache," she said. "I think I'll have to take a pill."

"Well, don't take it yet," I cried, closing the door quickly. I began to undress but had trouble with my combinations. Queenie, meanwhile, emerged out of the bathroom wearing an ankle length Wincyette nightdress, puce woollen bedsocks and a cloth nightcap hiding a row of protruding curlers.

I hopped towards her. "You look ravishing, my little flower."

"Oh Walter, you wouldn't bother me tonight would you, with my headache?"

"But Queenie, it's been so long."

"And it will be again, Walter, just you wait and see."

"But I've waited all this time. We may never get another chance like this." I managed to free my left leg and hopped onto my left foot to try to release the other leg but the wool caught on my big toe nail. "It won't take a minute," I cried.

"That's what I'm afraid of," said Queenie. "A long, slow night of passion is more my requirement. If, of course, I hadn't got this untimely headache."

At last, the combinations came off and I threw them to the floor. "I think you'll find your headache might disappear," I said softly, and sat on the edge of the bed, stroking her cheek gently. "That's better isn't it?" I leant down and kissed her lips. The effect was dramatic. She leapt to her feet and tore off the Wincyette nightdress. "It's obvious you only want me for my body."

"No, no. It's you I want. I do care for you, Queenie."

"Come on then, get on with it." She hurled her bedsocks across the room and lay naked and spreadeagled on the bed, her veins standing out in temper. I was reminded of the savoury ducks in the butcher's window. "Well, what are you waiting for?"

It was at that moment that all desire left me. Queenie was not slow to notice.

"Hah," she said scornfully. "All the fuss you've made about getting me here and now you can't manage it."

"I've been a victim of mental castration," I said. "It's never happened to me before. None of my previous wives perpetrated this cruel act of aggression."

"They didn't stay around long enough," she retorted. "What happened to your last one?"

"She was lured away from me by an Asian baggage handler who seduced her with false promises of free travel on Singapore Airlines."

"I think you'd better get under the clothes," said Queenie. "You could very easily get frostbite in your state of exposure."

I remembered the film extra searching for his frozen organ on the cobbles of imitation Belfast and pulled on my thermal vest and nightshirt. "I shall bid you goodnight," I said haughtily.

Found it hard to get to sleep for worrying about ways I could sneak out of the hotel leaving Queenie to pay the bill.

SUN FEB 17TH

Didn't wake until 10 a.m., to find that Queenie had upped and left. On the pillow next to me was my train ticket and the copy of Practical Poultry Keeper on which she had written 'so you won't feel lonely on the journey home'.

Dressing quickly, I ran downstairs to question the landlady.

"I'm afraid Mrs Molotov has gone on before you," she said.

"Dead, you mean?"

"Not dead, no. She said she had an urgent appointment with her astrologer and that you would settle the bill with me, Mr Molotov. Oh, and she said would you take her case back into town with you. She couldn't lift it on her own, poor soul."

"Well, I can't take it, not with my rupture ready to break out at any time."

"I'm afraid if you leave it, there will be a storage charge. In advance." She handed me an invoice.

The stairs nearly did for me on the upstairs climb. I collapsed on the bed gasping. "Did you want anything, sir?" enquired the chambermaid who had come to clean out the room.

"Only oxygen." I dragged Queenie's case from out of her wardrobe and put my toothbrush and nightshirt into my Marks and Spencers carrier bag. "And maybe you could get a lift installed as well."

I staggered down again, Queenie's case clattering on every stair. The landlady was waiting at the bottom.

"I want to query this bill," I said. "Bed and breakfast is only £20, it says so on the wall."

"The extra £7 is for the bar. Mrs Molotov came down again last night and availed herself of several port and lemons in the company of ladies from the Margate Pensioners Against Rape Society."

Due to the Sunday train services, it took me seven hours to get home. By this time I was suffering from hallucinations with tiredness. I left Queenie's case in the left luggage office at Margate Station.

As I stood on the landing, trying to hold my door key in my feeble grasp, Ron Alley appeared—putting his milk bottles out.

"I'm giving up women," I announced

"A bit late to tell me that, Walter," he said. "I've got Mrs Newfoundland now."

MON FEB 18TH

Woke with a pounding headache, streaming nose and breath like a skunk's armpit. When I tried to crawl out of bed for the Vic Inhaler, dizziness overcame me and I fell over. On hands and knees, I scrambled to the door and across the landing to knock up Mrs Newfoundland.

Her expression showed some surprise as she regarded me on her doormat on my knees. "It's too late to offer yourself now, Mr Sherlock. I've got Mr Alley."

I tried to stand up but trod on the end of my flannelette pyjamas that I bought to celebrate VE Day. The cord having lost its elasticity, they dropped to my feet.

Mrs Newfoundland viewed my newly exposed personal regions with some disdain. "I hope you don't think a little thing like that will help me change my mind."

"It's the cold weather."

"Perhaps you should keep it in a matchbox wrapped in cotton wool," and she shut the door.

Bravely, I knocked again. "I'm ill," I wheezed. "Please seek medical attention for me without delay."

She glared at me. "You've only got a cold, man. Pull yourself together."

"It could be malaria. I was in Australia during the Great War."

"Oh, very well," she relented. "Crawl back to your bed and I'll telephone for a doctor."

"You can't be too careful at 84," I advised her. "So, while you're at it, you'd better mobilise Meals on Wheels and a Home Help for me."

"Don't you have any relations?"

I thought of Marge and Neville but the prospect of a week of force-fed Spotted Dick put me off. "They're all in Whitehaven," I lied. "Second cousins. Big in nuclear fission." I started to cry. "I'm all alone in the world."

"You shouldn't be on your own in your condition, Mr Sherlock. You should be put into an institution."

"No, thank you. I couldn't stand custard every day."

Dr Gavin arrived within the hour. "Not again," was all the greeting he could manage. Whatever happened to the bedside manner? Medical students ought to be made to watch 30 hours of Dr Finlay before qualifying.

"It's been nearly a fortnight," I said.

"So long? You could have been dead and nobody told us."

"I think it's double pneumonia," I offered helpfully, "but we may have caught it in time."

"Really! No need to send for the Priest then?"

"I've been converted. The Jehovah's Witnesses came to the door."

"That's the end of your blood transfusions then. Do you want a credit note for the pint we owe you? You could use it for extra wart ointment perhaps."

"I didn't join them. They put the fear of God up me, as it were, and in my terror I turned to the Methodists. I've become a Calvinist Primitive. We meet in Abraham Lane Chapel with the corrugated roof on alternate Sundays and discuss the wrath of the Lord over a cup of tea and soft digestive biscuits. Then we sing Ancient and Modern hymns till closing time and the temptation of strong drink is passed."

He tapped his fingers against my chest, ordering me to breathe deeply.

"Not so hard, you'll crack my ribs."

"Perfectly clear. All you need is a packet of Mentholyptus and some fresh air. Why don't you take a day at the seaside?"

"It's because of a day at the seaside I'm in this state."

Yet again, I'm let down by the medical profession. If I was in BUPA they'd have sent me to Switzerland for a month now.

The Meals on Wheels arrived at noon bearing aluminium containers of Spotted Dick and Custard and Scrag End of Lamb.

I survived the day on a spare packet of unsalted peanuts.

TUES FEB 19TH

I am writing this locked in the joint bathroom. My room has been taken over by small children (the worst kind) who have been dumped on me by their mother, Paulette, who is the youngest of the six children I produced during my third marriage (to Moaning Mildred 1954-60).

Paulette has now got five children of her own and, typical of this age of obsolescence, has never used the same father twice. She lives in the lap of luxury in a Brixton basement flat courtesy of the DHSS, coincidentally my own benefactors.

She arrived on my doorstep first thing with the news that she was having to go into a Clapham clinic for the weekend for her Spring abortion, a regular event since her television was repossessed three years ago.

"Why won't your mother take them?" I protested. But it appeared that

Moaning Mildred had disowned her daughter after Paulette had used her mother's third husband to father her second child, Begley.

"So we've come to you, Pop," she said. I winced. The relationships were all too complicated for me and being called Pop made me feel like a blackcurrant cordial. Besides, I hadn't heard from Paulette for about 15 years and felt the imposition of her children was a trifle presumptuous.

But she knew how to get round me. "I'll slip you a bluey, Pop, for all the trouble. Now, here's the kids' medicines." She handed me a carrier bag containing an assortment of lotions, pills and mixtures.

"Aubrey has the thick pink stuff. You rub it on his chest for his rash. The yellow and black tablets are for Genevieve. She has two every three hours or three every two hours. I suppose it works out the same in the end."

I examined them. "They look a bit big." I rolled the bulbous confections in my hand.

"No, they're her liquorice allsorts." She produced a bottle of what looked like dead wasps. "These are her tablets. She's having painful periods."

"No wonder, at seven and a half."

"Genevieve's thirteen, silly. It's Sebastian who's eight and a half. His is the heliotrope ointment. It's for his lice. In fact, you can give them all a rub of that. They've probably all got them by now. Just in their hair."

"On their heads you mean?"

"No. Anywhere they have hair."

"Your mother's family used to grow hair in the most unsuspected places. Her sister had the hairiest shoulders I've seen outside the Brooke Bond TV adverts."

"You'll just have to search for all the hair you can find then. Now then, what have we left? Oh yes, the linctus." She rummaged in the carrier and withdrew a bottle of light brown liquid. I took out the cork and sniffed.

"Doesn't smell so bad. Cough mixture is it?"

She scrutinised the label. "Oh dear, my mistake. That's our Begley's sample to take to the doctor's. I wonder how it got in here. How long have you been taking this, Clover?"

"She had some yesterday, Mam," shouted Sebby gleefully.

"Oh well, it's not done her any harm and her cough's certainly better. I might give it her again."

"What about Begley? Won't the doctor be waiting for his sample?"

"I shouldn't think so. I've probably sent them Clover's linctus by mistake. It'll be interesting to see what they make of that."

Sebby tugged urgently at his mother's sleeve. He looked like an extra from 'Hard Times', a shabby urchin. "Mam, I've gorra lump in me 'ead."

"How can it be *in* your head?" I asked. "Growing in your brain is it?"

He glared. "It's in me 'air. Feel."

His mother felt, then lifted up a thick pile of greasy hair. "I think it's a nest," she declared. "I think we've found the nesting place of the lice. Give me that spray in the carrier. That should do for the little beggars."

"What about the ointment?" I said.

"This'll be stronger, it's insecticide. Finish 'em off in no time."

I glimpsed the label. "It says for garden use only."

"We'll take them in the garden then. Sebby's hair grows like one anyway." She grabbed her son by the collar. "I think we could do to hack a bit of this off."

"I've got an old saw somewhere," I said. "I'd cut the lot off. It'd be far healthier and I've got a couple of cushions that need filling."

Paulette took the lid off the insecticide. Sebby screamed and ran out of the door, nearly decapitating Mrs Newfoundland who was passing on the landing with a cup of hot Complan for Mr Alley who has been feeling the strain of her constant demands.

"I'll get him later," said Paulette, replacing the lid. "He'll be back for his tea."

"Pity about the hair," I said. "Foam is very uncomfortable in cushions, it springs back at you when you lie on it. I've had whiplash injuries from that settee."

"They like fresh, wholesome food, Pop. I usually give them chicken livers, lambs heart, lots of chips and sausages and salted crisps."

"If they stay with me, they'll get nut rissoles and like it." The time had come, I felt, to assert myself. "And if you're not back by tomorrow night from this unwholesome excursion, then I shall leave them at the Police Station."

Paulette left shortly afterwards. I have been in the bathroom thirty minutes, steeling myself to come out. It is now 8 p.m. so I shall have to move soon as two of them will have to sleep in the bath. How lucky that Mrs Newfoundland and Mr Alley only bathe on alternate Saturdays.

WED FEB 20TH

A sleepless night. In the end, it was I who had to sleep in the bath, the children locking themselves in my room. Sebby made a hammock out of my curtains and slung it between the bedposts and the curtain rail. Clover slept in it, she being the lightest. Unfortunately, she is also the incontinent one and, whilst the stains on the carpet may come out, I am not so optimistic about the curtains.

Clover is one of the most irritating people I know. She screams incessantly like a mating corncrake until her ears go purple and she stops breathing. She has a habit of throwing her dummy on the floor, waiting for you to pick it up then spitting at you and throwing it down again.

This morning, I had to take them with me to the Post Office to collect my pension. Hardly had we got down the street before Clover threw the dummy away. Furious, I kicked it into the gutter where it fell down a grid.

"That'll stop your antics, you odious little pillock."

Clover started her familiar scream. "You'd better get it back," Begley advised me.

"Certainly not. She'll have to learn to live without it."

Now Begley joined in the screaming. "Fetch the NSPCC," he bellowed. One or two passers-by stopped to look.

I gave in. "All right, I'll get it." Trying to look casual, I knelt in the gutter and stretched my fingers through the filthy bars of the grid towards the dummy floating in the dark mire a good foot below.

"What's going on?" enquired a curious bystander.

Begley tapped his head sadly. "Poor old bugger's got bad eyesight. Thinks he's robbing a charity wishing well."

I couldn't reach the dummy. "She'll have to have Sebastian's instead," I said, but he refused to remove it from his mouth. "You *are* eight and a half, Sebastian," I pointed out. "Won't people think you're a bit strange having a dummy still?"

"He *is* a bit strange," said Genevieve.

Aubrey smiled secretly. "Do you know something we don't?" I asked him.

Aubrey brought a tube from his pocket. "Superglue," he announced. "I got fed up of sniffing it so I put some on Sebby's dummy. It'll be stuck in there till next Christmas."

"Just as well," I said. "He always did have too much to say. We might as well leave it in."

"I want my dummy back," screamed Clover. The crowd still hovered; then, on the horizon, I spotted a bus. "Quick children, let's get the bus to town," I cried and they all ran for the stop. I hobbled behind them, relieved at escaping what could have been an ugly scene, but worse was to come.

The children spread about the bus and I collapsed exhausted on the back seat. Hardly had we started moving before Aubrey came rushing down the aisle grinning. "Begley's showing his winkle to the lady in the green hat."

98

I jumped up and went to investigate. Surely enough, Begley was holding it in his hand like a pink worm and waving it at his companion who stared steadfastly out of the side window.

"Put it away, Begley," said Genevieve who had come across to look. "It's a pathetic specimen anyway."

"It's growing," smiled Begley, with satisfaction.

"Oh my God!" I said. The lady grimaced but continued to keep her head averted.

Clover, meanwhile, on the front seat, had relieved a partially-sighted pensioner of his wallet and trotted down the bus with it, smiling triumphantly. "Here you are," she said, handing it to me like a trained Faginite.

"She's only 3½," said Aubrey, shaking his head. "There ought to be posters warning strange middle aged men to keep away from little girls like Clover."

The conductor appeared, dragging Sebby along by his collar. "Is this yours?" he enquired. "Only, when I invited him to purchase a ticket, he tried to jump off."

"Never seen him before." We all spoke in unison.

"Why has that strange boy got a dummy in his mouth?" asked Clover, but the conductor had turned his attentions to Begley who was still exhibiting his tumescent organ with the air of a horticulturist who knows his is the prize marrow.

"Madam," he addressed the lady in the green hat. "Kindly get your child to desist."

"My child!" echoed the lady. "I've never seen him before, the filthy animal."

Begley threw his arms round her neck. "Mummy, how could you!" he cried.

"Both of you, off this bus immediately."

"Quite right too," I enjoined. "You ought to be ashamed of yourself, Madam, allowing such behaviour in public. I shouldn't have to witness such spectacles at 84."

"I tell you, he's not mine. He just sat next to me and exposed himself."

"A likely story," I said. "This sort of thing wouldn't have happened in Disraeli's time. Morals are too lax nowadays."

The conductor, having abandoned his attempt to expel the offenders from his vehicle, turned his attention to the collection of revenue. "Fares please," he shouted.

Genevieve answered him by reaching up and slapping him hard across the face. "Stop trying to look down my dress," she cried. "I'm only 13, you dirty sod. You should be incarcerated." The conductor went a bright red, a remarkable achievement for an Indian. Sebby took advantage of the diversion, broke away from the conductor's grasp and kicked his shin viciously. Genevieve slapped his face again. "Molester," she bawled. "In charge of a public service vehicle too."

Begley glanced up from his manipulations. "Let's see yours," he smiled at the conductor.

The pensioner on the front seat stood up to scream, "Somebody's stole my wallet."

"That little girl was sitting next to him," said a passenger pointing at Genevieve.

"I'll follow her," said Genevieve and ran for the exit door which fortuitously opened as the bus reached the terminus. I made my way down the aisle.

"What about your fare?" the conductor demanded.

"How dare you," I said, "after an exhibition like that? I've a good mind to report you to the Raj."

"Children wouldn't have behaved like that when I was at school," commented the lady in the green hat. "There's too much violence in society nowadays."

"Quite," I agreed. "When I was at school, it was the masters who were violent, not the children. When we misbehaved, we were sent to the gym to do the splits."

"And did that cure you?"

"No. It was just their way of recruiting sopranos for the school choir."

"Really!" She stalked off, unamused. I gathered the children and, after I'd collected my pension, I walked them home then locked them in the room with me to ensure none of them escaped before Paulette's return.

Paulette didn't arrive till midnight and she had a man in tow. "This is Fergus," she slurred, obviously the worse for drink. Fergus had a wild beard, stained with Stones' Bitter, missing teeth and the stomach of a professional darts player.

He leaned forward to shake my hand, swayed and was sick on the carpet.

"Fergus can play 'The Entertainer' on the bassoon," remarked Paulette unnecessarily.

"Luckily, we only have a French Horn available," I said. "Begley, wake up. There's some sick for you to mop up. And hurry; I'm expecting the Health Inspector at dawn."

"Have they been much trouble?" Paulette asked. "Only I wouldn't mind leaving them another couple of months while I find a new flat."

"I want them out in three minutes or I'll call the Police."

Paulette shrugged. "Oh well, we'll have to stay with Fergus. He's got a caravan at Stepney."

They left shortly afterwards. I searched them each at the door. Sebby still had his dummy but Paulette seemed unconcerned. "We've stuck one in his mouth before. It stops him eating so much. Crisps are so expensive nowadays aren't they?"

I have 32 grandchildren. I will happily die without seeing the other 27.

THURS FEB 21ST

Back to the dentist's this morning. Ms Bennett looked as ravishing as ever despite the lethal instruments of torture she held in her hand.

"I've only come for the impression," I warned her.

"We may as well make a start on the removal of your upper teeth," she said. "Six a month I think we agreed."

"But I'm not ready for it. I need to work myself up into a state of morbid terror."

"I think I'll do the front ones first, they'll be easier. They've nearly rotted away as it is."

Before I could protest further, she had the needle in my gum, and the operation was under way. The six teeth came out with the usual accompanying pain, little alleviated by the injection.

"Should I throw them away or will you be making them into a necklace to ward off evil spirits?" smiled Ms Bennett, rattling them around in her hand like dice.

"They look a bit like my gallstones," I said. "I've got them in a jar on my mantelpiece at home. Pickled."

"Why not throw the teeth in as well then? Let them swim around together. Who knows, as more bits of you drop off, it could make for an interesting collection." She collected a lump of pink Plasticine from the bench. "Now open up Mr Sherlock, I'll just get the impression of your gums for your lower dentures."

Without warning, she stuffed the substance into my mouth and pressed it viciously towards my epiglottis. I choked and gagged but she held firm against my gum until it set hard.

"Call back in a week," she said, "and next time, try not to be sick on my hand."

Arrived back at the flat with a sore mouth and was quite unable to eat the

101

nut cutlet I had saved for my lunch. In the end, I had to soak it in hot water, grind it and drink it as soup. Hardly had I finished the nourishing beverage before the doorbell rang.

"Who is it?" I lisped through my newly exposed gums.

"It's Mrs O'Leary from Computer Dating." The voice was Irish. So she had arrived, but what an unfortunate time to call.

"Who do you want?" I cried out weakly. "There's no Mr Sherlock here."

"Is that you, Mr Sherlock?" came the unmistakable voice of Mrs Newfoundland. "There's a lady here for you."

Resignedly, I opened the door. The woman who confronted me was a hideous sight. She was built like a Greek colossus with the shoulders of a prop forward and a ginger wig sitting slightly off-centre on her undersized, pea-like head.

For a moment she stood and looked me up and down. "You've aged since your photograph was taken. A good 60 years in fact." She pushed past me and set her shopping bag down on the table. "And acquired a new leg, I see."

I was not in a position to deny it. The leg was not something I could have borrowed from a friend. "It was the only photo I had," I explained.

"I've been with Computer Dating eight years now, Mr Sherlock. I'm used to people's little deceptions. Most men send photographs of Cary Grant and Stewart Grainger."

"Eight years?" I repeated. "And you've had no success in finding a suitable partner to offer you a lifetime of happiness and contentment as promised in the company's expensive brochures?"

"I'm not looking for a lifetime partner, Mr Sherlock. I'm looking for an endless supply of men who will escort me to expensive restaurants, take me on exotic holidays and worship me with their bodies. I work on an average of a month for each man."

I regarded her closely and decided that even the last criterion would not be possible. "In that case," I said, "put me down for a year next December. It'll give me time to build my strength up."

"Are you telling me that I am not what you are looking for?"

"I certainly am, madam. I specifically requested West Indian ladies. I happen to be a closet Rastafarian."

And with that, I escorted her to the door. I feel I have had a narrow escape. The whole computer idea has been a waste of time and money. In future, I shall stick to chatting up the late stragglers in the Wednesday pension queue.

FRI FEB 22ND

Natalie arrived this morning on her way to the swimming baths. She wanted to borrow £2 for her lunch with the Wimmin Against Heterosexuality in Primary Schools Group.

"Why don't you come swimming with me, Walter?" she said. "It'd do you good; build up your muscle."

I explained that I couldn't swim. "That is, I can manage three strokes but the third one always takes me to the bottom."

"I'll teach you," she offered. "Think of all the topless sunbathers on the beaches at Majorca. You'll be able to join them once you learn to swim."

It was a powerful argument but I hesitated. "What about my morbid fear of drowning?"

"I won't let you drown," she promised. "Get your costume out and we'll go."

"Can't I leave my combinations on? It'll be chilly in the public baths. The council can't afford the coke to keep the boilers going."

"And what would you wear to come home in? Now, don't be silly and get your costume."

I allowed myself to be persuaded. "Still got the Robin Reliant," I said as we got to the car. "Do you use the sou'wester I gave you or have you got a garage for it now?"

"Very funny," she said. "Jump in." She turned the key in the ignition but the engine failed to fire.

"Perhaps it's run out of petrol," I said. "Do you want me to get a cupful from the garage?"

She ignored me and slammed her foot on the accelerator which had the desired effect of jerking the engine into life.

"Nippy little beggar," I commented as we moved down the street. "If you put your foot down we might catch that old lady up before the lights. Good job she's got the shopping trolley though to slow her down."

"Have you never had swimming lessons before?" Natalie changed the subject.

"Only at school. But the teacher believed the important thing was to conquer our fear of water so he had us picking up bricks from the bottom of the pool to get us used to getting our heads underwater."

"Did it work?"

"Well, we never learnt any strokes so we could none of us swim, but if we drowned we'd do it calmly and with dignity."

Natalie snorted. "I'll get you swimming, don't worry." We reached the baths and I allowed myself to be led in. "Go and get changed," Gnat

103

instructed, "and I'll meet you in the main pool in five minutes."

It took me ten minutes to struggle out of my thermal underwear and into the costume and Natalie was not impressed when I finally appeared. "For God's sake, Walter, what have you got on? They stopped wearing those striped bathing suits in 1920."

"I haven't been in the water since 1920. Besides, I see no reason to arouse the unbridled passions of comparative strangers by appearing virtually naked in a public arena."

"But what are those two pink things dangling underneath it?"

"Those are my knees. What did you think they were?"

"I'm not quite sure," she said doubtfully. "I haven't got your geography right yet. I mean, are those things at the bottom of your legs really ankles? They look thin enough to be fingers to me. And those red things on them, are they boils or what?"

"They are my water wings, my only form of life saving equipment."

"But you don't need them on your ankles as well as your arms. You'll be floating away like Mary Poppins. Anyway, come on down into the water and see how you go. At least you're not afraid of getting your head wet."

"I get it wet most days the amount of rain we've been having." I stepped gingerly down the ladder and waded towards her.

"Right, stand up then, Walter."

"I AM standing up. It's deep in here, you know."

She looked down. "Oh, so you are. Right, now I want you to put both your arms forward then slowly lean onto the water."

I did so. "Help, I'm drowning," I cried and struggled to my feet.

"How can you drown when the water only comes up to your neck?"

"That's when I'm standing. When I lie down, it comes to two feet above my head."

"Try floating on your back instead."

I lay back but my head immediately disappeared under the water causing me to choke. Bubbles rose to the surface. "Ugh," I spat. "Have you tasted that? It's full of chloroform."

"Chlorine, Walter. Chloroform would put you to sleep which, come to think of it, may not be such a bad idea. If they didn't put chlorine in the water, we'd all be poisoned. Only last week, there was something very unpleasant floating in this pool but, before I could complain to the attendant, someone had swallowed it."

"You don't mean people might actually spit in this water do you?" I asked in horror. "Only I read in the Sunday Times that you can catch Aids from spit."

"Don't forget that most of the junior class of the Reginald Kray Comprehensive School have probably relieved themselves in this water already this morning." Gnat grinned cheerfully. "Anyway, it'd be the only way you'd ever catch Aids at your advanced age."

"What do you mean by that?" I cried but, in my indignation, my foot slipped and my head went under again, causing me to swallow another mouthful of the putrid fluid. I spat it out quickly.

"Look," said Natalie. "Why don't you hold onto the edge and practise a few strokes? When you feel confident you can let go. God knows, with all those balloons you've got strapped to you, you can hardly sink."

I did as she instructed but no amount of threshing seemed to propel me forward.

"I think your problem, Walter, is weak wrists. Do you ever exercise them at all?"

"It's not my wrists, it's my arms. They're too thin to move all that heavy water."

"Walter, this is the shallow end of the Dennis Lotis Swimming Baths, not the Red Sea. Perhaps you'd better go in the children's pool if these giant waves are too much for you."

"I wish this was the Red Sea. Moses never had this trouble."

"Maybe you need weight training. If you were a bit stronger you might be able to propel yourself through the water."

I shook my head. "No thanks. I've had enough. I think I might take up poker instead, that's more my sort of sport. Good exercise too, all that shuffling and dealing. Keeps your thumbs active."

"Don't give up, Walter. I'll get you swimming."

"You'd have more chance getting Linda Lovelace elected Pope."

"But what about your Majorcan holiday?"

"I've decided to go to Walsall instead. There's fewer beaches in Walsall."

SAT FEB 23RD

Arranged to go to the football match with Jim Evans this afternoon so spent the morning ironing my Everton scarf for the occasion. Couldn't find my rattle but remembered I'd given it to Mrs Newfoundland to frighten off double glazing salesmen as Mr Murray would not allow her to keep a dog.

Partook of a particularly disagreeable meal at Marge and Neville's at lunch-time. Apart from the unimaginative stodginess of the fare (non-macrobiotic suet dumplings, burnt Oxo and scrag ends of mutton floating

105

in big globules of fat just waiting to get in there and clog your arteries), the atmosphere was akin to the court room at the Nuremberg Trials. Nobody can burn an Oxo cube like Marge, which is why Neville has taken to eating at the Conservative Club most days. That, and the promise of a nostalgic grope with his erstwhile mistress behind the lifesize icon of Mrs Thatcher in the voting chamber.

During the meal, there was a row about my contribution to the household expenses. "Why should I bring anything?" I objected. "I don't live here."

"You bring your horrible washing here. You're always coming here for meals. I think you should offer something towards the cost. Persil's not as cheap as it used to be."

"Use soap then. It was good enough for Neville's mother."

"Neville's mother probably did her washing with stones by the side of the canal. Persil wouldn't have been much good in the canal. They've invented washing machines now. Come on, you miser, just £5. You can afford it."

"I've only got my pension."

"What about this legacy you're always going on about or is that just another ugly rumour like the suggestion that you have a bath more than once a month?"

"My skin's sensitive to the allergies in bath cubes. Anyway, that money is all tied up for my descendants. Those of whom I choose to leave it to, that is."

"And it won't be long before they get it either, going to the football match in this weather at your time of life. 84's a funny age, you know. I hope you've got your thermal jock strap on."

"The spectators don't wear jock straps, woman. It's only the players that have a uniform."

"Could've fooled me with that blue and white woollen hat and that blue and white striped scarf and those blue and white socks. I bet you've dyed your rupture belt blue and white as well."

I didn't stay for the pudding which, I believe, was the usual Spotted Dick. I sometimes think Marge must have once had a lover with warts and she is trying to recreate his memory with these confections, like sponge monuments.

Jim Evans looked at me strangely when we met outside the ground. "What's the matter?" I asked. "My shirt tails aren't hanging out, are they?"

He scratched a suppurating pustule on his forehead. "Er, should you be wearing that blue and white scarf, Walter? It is Tottenham we're going to watch."

"It might be Tottenham you're watching, Jim but, personally, I'll be supporting Everton. I like that Dixie Dean."

"Walter, it's 50 years since Dixie Dean was playing."

"It's 50 years since I've seen them. They've had time to find a decent replacement by now." I thrust my way into a queue. "Come on, let's get in here."

"We're only just in time," said Jim Evans, as we got into the ground. "The ref's blowing his whistle any second. I must say, I'd've preferred to go in the Stands. Two hours is a long time to be standing in this cold."

"Don't worry about it. It's so packed in here that you won't fall over even if you do faint with exposure."

Jim looked around then nudged me. "Hey, Walter, there seems to be a lot of buggers with blue scarves round here."

"That's because we're in the Everton Enclosure. I'd take that Spurs hat off if I was you."

"Oh Hell." He stuffed his bobble hat into his pocket. "Now I'll get chilblains on my head." His scarf followed the hat. "I'm freezing now."

"You should get a Balaclava like me. Keeps the icy blasts out a treat."

Jim Evans looked decidedly miserable, a mood not improved by the half-time score of 2-0 to Everton.

"Eh up, Walter," he said suddenly. "It's started to rain."

I put out my hand, "No it's not."

"I distinctly felt something wet trickling down the back of my shoe."

I turned round furtively. "You're all right, Jim," I whispered. "It's not raining. The fellow behind couldn't make it through the crowd to the Gents, that's all. We're OK."

Jim Evans didn't look OK. He started to shout "Come on you Spurs", when his team ran out for the second half but received such malevolent glares from our neighbours that he was forced to cheer for Everton in order to insure himself against assault and battery. Everton scored two more goals.

The result not being in their favour, the rest of the crowd around the ground turned ugly and waved abuse at our little section.

"Don't worry," a policeman on the touchline assured us. "They can't get at you. We've locked you safely in until your coach comes round to take you back to Liverpool."

"Hang on," shouted Jim Evans. "We don't want to go to Liverpool. We live here."

"Fifth columnists, eh?" shouted an Everton supporter gleefully.

"You shouldn't be in there then," retorted the policeman.

107

"You're coming back with us now, la'," said the Scouser. "I hope you like Ken Dodd."

"Get us out," I shouted to the policeman. "I'm 84. I need hospital treatment every six hours."

"Aw, piss off, you gobshite," roared the Everton supporter.

"Don't you call me a gobshite, you dickhead," I shouted and took out my pension book to wave at him.

"Hey, that's an offensive weapon," they yelled. "Arrest him, constable."

Someone threw a golf ball. It hit Jim Evans on the head, right on his pimple. He slumped to the ground. I picked up the ball and threw it back into the Tottenham crowd whence it came. Unfortunately, hindered by my recurrent arthritis, my aim was bad and the ball hit the policeman instead.

The policeman immediately thundered towards me. "That's it. I saw that. You're under arrest."

I pointed to the recumbent figure of Jim Evans, still groaning on the ground, hands clasped to his forehead. "It was him, officer. I saw him throw it."

"I saw you throw it, now just come with me."

"Quite right," said the Everton supporter. "You lock him up. Old beggars like him give the game a bad name. No wonder us teenagers are frightened to go to football matches without our mothers with people like him about." He spat on Jim Evans and turned away. He was six foot two with a Mohican haircut and bondage leggings.

The charge was something about causing a riot. I am writing this from a police cell in Hackney.

SUN FEB 24TH

Spent a distressing night in prison, locked up with a crowd of Tottenham supporters who made short work of my Everton scarf and hat.

It was lunchtime before Marge, alerted by Jim Evans, arrived to bail me out. "You're a disgrace to the family," she complained. "I've told Neville we might have to change our name."

When I got back to the flat, Mr Murray, the landlord, accosted me in the porch. "You're back then, Mr Sherlock. Only there's been a woman looking for you. Well not a woman, exactly."

"What do you mean, 'exactly'?" I said. "Either she was a woman or she wasn't.'

"She was a nun."

"Not collecting, was she?" I asked apprehensively. Once your name gets

108

on some of these mailing lists, the begging letters and the gift envelopes arrive by every post.

"No. She said she'd been given your name by some agency. Sister Maria-Theresa she was called. She seemed to be expecting to marry you Mr Sherlock." His eyes glinted. "I hope you realise you are only paying single terms for your room."

The Computer Dating Agency! How long will this go on? What if that Horatio creature should call? Why didn't I give them Jim Evans' address?

MON FEB 25TH

What a horrific night! I have been taken for a night on the town by Natalie and I never want to leave my flat again unless Nuclear War strikes. Perhaps it was my punishment for not learning to swim.

She arrived after tea and announced she was taking me for what she called a 'treat'. I reminded her of an earlier 'treat' when I was arrested at the Miners' Demo in the town centre. "We won't be going to Wapping, for instance?" I asked. "Only I have no quarrel with that Mr Murdoch. I buy The Sun religiously every morning for its in-depth news coverage and unbiased political commentary."

"Liar," said Natalie. "You buy it for the Page Three boobs which we feminists are anxious to stamp out. Only because, at your age, you've forgotten what they look like."

This was regrettably true. The last naked woman I had seen was in the X-Ray Department at the Louis Armstrong Infirmary for Geriatrics two years ago. I was waiting for the results of an investigation into the workings of my lower colon when an old lady of about 110, dressed in a white sheet and matching label as if ready for the morgue, slipped on the polished floor. As she clattered to the ground, the sheet fell from her revealing a display of red hanging skin and blue veins that bore no relation to the pictures in The Sun.

"Just as long as we're not going near that electric fence. Those printers can be quite as violent as the miners were."

"Walter. This is a fun night out. No demonstrations, no protest meetings, no Wapping."

"I've got to be in bed early," I warned her, "on account of my low blood pressure. My heart stops pumping for the day round about midnight so I need to be lying down by then to keep it swilling round until morning when it starts up again."

"I've never heard so much rubbish. Listen, Walter, I'm going to give you a good time."

Now I was worried. The last time a woman promised me a good time, she stole my trousers. They never caught her and I lost £3.26p, a packet of Dentyne chewing gum and my life membership for the Edward Heath Indoor Amusement Centre.

"Are we going far?" I enquired. "Will I need to put my Thermogen on?"

"Only into town. If you must know, I've got us tickets for a concert."

"Not at the end of the pier I hope. My Wellingtons let water in."

"It's at the Odeon. Have you heard of Gary Glitter?"

"Of course I have. That's the stuff you clean silver with, like Brasso." Natalie grimaced. "He's a singer, you berk."

"He's not a teenage idol is he? Only, I don't want to be trodden on by hordes of squealing children."

"They'll all be students, it's a college do. Now get your coat and come on."

The theatre was packed. There were not many octogenarians in the audience though; in fact I spotted nobody I knew from the Over 60's. When the band came on, I realised why. The noise was so great that my hearing aid leapt out of my ear and I could still hear every note.

"Once the Hard of Hearing Club know about this," I shouted, "they'll be cancelling their annual pilgrimage to Lourdes and come here instead."

"Shush," screamed Gnat.

"What do you mean, 'shush' in this lot?" I yelled.

"It's Gary!" A portly figure took to the stage dressed like a pregnant fairy on a Christmas tree. He jumped from leg to leg as if troubled by chronic constipation. I knew how he felt.

"Liquid paraffin could help him," I shouted to Natalie but my words were drowned by a raucous din as he started to sing. "Why is he waving his arms like that? If he wants to leave the stage, he can just go."

Natalie ignored me and started to sing along with the song. "I'm the leader, I'm the leader . . ."

"He must be getting on," I bawled. "Poor old bugger. Fancy having to do this for a living at his age. He ought to apply to the council. They should be able to find him something in the Parks and Cemeteries Department. On second thoughts though, perhaps not. With a voice like that, he might wake the dead."

"I wish you'd be more grateful," shouted Natalie. "There's people locked outside this theatre who'd've given good money for your ticket."

"Where? Take me to them," I cried. "Spivs are they? Representatives of all the finest values of our capitalist society." Before Natalie could reply, I

was halfway up the gangway. She was right. I got £10 for my torn ticket from a white person of indeterminate sex with an earring in its nose, glittering among the acne scabs.

I spent £1 of my new found wealth on a taxi home. I asked the driver to turn the radio down only to find it wasn't on. "You've had one too many, Grandad," he said. "Old tearaways like you should be in bed at night with your Bible and your teeth in a clean tumbler of water instead of drinking and gambling at all night bingo dens."

"I've been to see Gary Glitter," I explained, "and I can still hear him."

"Gary Glitter? Is he the American evangelist preacher?"

"Quarter past nine," I answered.

He gave up.

The ringing in my ears persisted all night, almost drowning out the cries of passion from Mrs Newfoundland and Mr Alley wafting through the paper thin walls.

TUES FEB 26TH

Woke in confusion thinking the alarm had gone off but it was just the late tinnitus after last night's concert. Even the solid wall of wax, carefully built up over the years to protect my eardrums against the sound of Marge's incessant moans, had failed to keep out the awesome sound of the Grand Old Trouper.

Luckily, down the side of the bed settee I found a water pistol left by one of Paulette's odious offspring so I decided to syringe my ears. I'd run out of Fairy Liquid so I had to make to with warm water with a dash of Bell's whisky for antiseptic effect. I held the pistol carefully to my left ear and was about to pull the trigger when Mrs Newfoundland came clattering through the door to the accompaniment of splintering wood.

"Don't do it, Mr Sherlock," she screamed, hurling her skeletal frame against me.

"For God's sake, woman." I dropped the water pistol and tried to avoid being cut by her sharp bones.

"We've been knocking for ten minutes then Mr Alley peeped through your letter box and saw you about to take your life. Is it financial troubles or news of an incurable wasting disease?"

"I was washing my ears out, you dolt," I replied.

Ron Alley trotted into the room holding his hand to his eye. "Let him top himself if he wants to, it's none of our business. The poor bugger's not long to go anyway, at his age."

"He was only washing his ears out," said Mrs Newfoundland. "What's the matter with your eye?"

"I got hit by flying splinters when you charged through that door like a battering ram."

"I shouldn't worry, Ron," I said. "You'll be able to manage on the one eye."

"What's all this noise up here?" Mr Murray, the landlord, appeared at the damaged doorway. He did not look a happy man. "Who's done this to my property?"

"Mr Alley here has had one of his attacks," I explained. "But we've given him his injection and he's calmed down now."

"I don't want vandals in my house. I knew it was a mistake taking in pensioners. You've never got the War out of your systems."

"I assure you the War was never in my system," I said. "I was a conscientious objector in the First and a listed deserter in the Second."

"But he'll be prepared to fight in the next one," Ron Alley assured him, "providing it's not against the Australians because it'd be too far for him to travel with his nervous asthma."

"It's highly unlikely we shall find ourselves in armed combat against Australia," murmured Mrs Newfoundland, "although if 'Bluey' is an example of their culture, it might not be a bad idea."

"I'll be sending my bill," snarled Mr Murray. "And while I'm here, I'd like a bit less noise from your rooms at night." He jerked his head in Ron Alley's direction. "These walls are paper thin and all that heaving and stuff you do disturbs the viewers in the television lounge. I'd be obliged if you'd restrict your marital obligations to the hours of ten to eleven o'clock on a Saturday night as the Radio Doctor recommends." He turned abruptly and left.

"Of course, we'll be getting our own place soon," said Mrs Newfoundland, "as soon as Ron gets his compensation."

"Oh, had an accident have you?"

"It's his finger. He trapped it in a machine at work. Severed the end completely. Nail and all."

"Blood everywhere," added Ron Alley.

"Couldn't you have had it sewn back on?" I asked. "They can do wonders with microsurgery nowadays."

"Precisely," said Ron Alley. "And where would that leave me? With ten perfect fingers and back at work in no time."

"Whereas," said Mrs Newfoundland, "without his finger, he gets early retirement, hefty compensation, a disablement pension and a red parking disc allowing him to ignore major traffic signals in overcrowded High Streets."

"So I managed to kick my finger down the drain when nobody was looking. I suppose I could have put it in my pocket and kept it as a souvenir, made into a key fob perhaps. But you don't think of those things at such moments of stress."

"Not with portions of your person rolling down the floor without you," I agreed. "Shall you be getting a replacement finger for cosmetic purposes?"

"That's what I told him," said Mrs Newfoundland. "A nice plastic one. Save him having to have his gloves specially made but he says having nine digits will give him the edge when he deals at the Whist Drive."

"It's his right index finger," I mused. "It's going to make it difficult for him to pick his nose. He'll never get that stump up his nostril in a million years."

"Tweezers, Walter. And I can manipulate them with my left hand, no danger."

Such remarkable ingenuity. Why have I never been able to turn my nervous asthma to such advantage?

In all the excitement, I forgot to syringe my ears and the ringing has come back.

WED FEB 27TH

Natalie called and offered to make my breakfast. I was careful not to request the Shredded Wheat in case it got mixed up with the cannabis again. Settled for the black puddings and prunes with a glass of Andrews to wash them down. Natalie assured me this would alleviate all my digestive problems causing what she called a Blaster Bates Reaction in my insides I wasn't too happy about the Andrews. The white powder bubbling away in the tumbler looked suspiciously like substances I've seen in Hill Street Blues sold for $120 a pinch. Still, if it was cocaine, I figured it would at least be good for my toothache.

"I'm taking you into town this morning, Walter," she informed me. "After Tuesday night, I've decided I've got to give you street credibility."

"Which street were you thinking of?"

"Be serious. You stood out like a virgin in a brothel at that concert last night. You need modernizing."

"I'm not a bathroom," I protested.

"It's your skin that's the problem, such a strange colour."

114

"I can't get a suntan in February. Anyway, I don't scrape my goose grease off until May."

"It needs decorating. Take the emphasis away from those purple veins and your horrible pouchy bits."

I had not been aware of any 'horrible pouchy bits" and informed Gnat in no uncertain terms that I was not taking to poncy bracelets and jewellery. What she had in mind, though, was something different.

"What you need, Walter, is a few tattoos. Very macho. We could inscribe the names of your wives across the back of your hands for starters."

"Better make that my fingers. It would give me room for another four. Hang on, though, won't this hurt?"

"No more than being branded with a red-hot poker like they do with sheep. But you're all right, they'll hold you down."

The tatooist was nineteen. He wore metal-studded armlets, denims and shoulder length hair. He produced a box of fierce looking needles.

"Just imagine you're at the acupuncturist's," said Natalie hastily when she saw the alarm on my face. "A prick in the right place could cure your nervous asthma or whatever it is you're always complaining about."

"And what if it's in the wrong place. I might get a lumbar puncture against my will."

"Nonsense. Show him your tattoos, Gerald."

Gerald pulled up his shirt to reveal the insignia of a heavy metal band on his hairless chest, tributes to his late mother on one arm and a record of his undying devotion to a girl named Mildred on the other. The latter sentiments vied with the inscription expressed on his back, his affection for Wanda J. who seemed to be a mermaid.

"Show him your bottom," insisted Natalie, and Gerald lowered his jeans obligingly. Beneath the inscription 'Dancing Cheek to Cheek' were portraits of a man and a lady, one on each buttock.

"Fred Astaire and Ginger Rogers?" I enquired, squinting hard at his denuded posterior.

"Mrs Thatcher actually," he said. "And the other one is King Kong. Two monsters you see."

"Not unlike Fred Astaire is he?" I murmured, turning away as Gerald reassembled his clothing. "He hasn't got any more to show us has he?" I pleaded. "In places we haven't seen?"

"I don't think so Walter."

"I've decided to have transfers, anyway," I said. "They're less painful."

Natalie refused to accept this. "Nonsense. We'll just have a couple of tiny ones on the back of your hands for starters. What do you fancy?

Swastikas? CND? Arsenal?"

"How about Samantha Fox?"

Natalie was not amused. "Really Walter. Making sexist remarks like that at your age, you should know better."

"What about Gerald's mermaid? Isn't that sexist?"

"That's wildlife, a totally different thing."

I agreed, mainly because you don't argue with Natalie. Gerald came across with a catalogue and asked me to choose a design and eventually I agreed on a pair of matching faces.

"Will he put me to sleep?" I asked.

"Only if you struggle," smiled Gerald, nastily. "Just put your wrists into these clamps and we'll get on with it."

I obeyed meekly. Twenty minutes later I was marked for life.

Natalie took me home to lie down after my ordeal. I had hoped for lunch but she explained I was better on an empty stomach after the tattooing. Besides, she only had 70p till dole day.

This evening I attended the Conservative Club Whist Drive. Much whispered comment was made about my hands, mainly behind my back.

"Mr Sherlock looks pale," I heard Old Mrs Pemberton say. "Has he been under the doctor?"

"They've got a new lady doctor at the health centre now," said Mrs Hargreaves. "More likely she's been under him. You know what Mr Sherlock's like!"

"Why is he wearing those white gloves? Does he think he's Liberace?"

"Perhaps he's been to a wedding. Mind you, he hasn't got a top hat to go with them."

"Well, it doesn't help him deal the cards. We had to wait ten minutes on that last table before Mrs Bumhold took over and she's got advanced arthritis in nine of her fingers. In the end we had to cut it off. There wasn't any time to play."

"We were just commenting on your attire, Mr Sherlock," said Mrs Hargreaves as she saw me glance her way. "Finding it cold in here with your circulation, are you? I suppose when I get to your age . . ." her voice trailed off scornfully.

"I am only eighty-four, madam, and my blood courses through my veins as vigorously as it always did." She nodded pityingly. "As a matter of fact, I had an operation on my hands this morning."

"Not your fingers, was it? How many did you have off? Was it gangrene? It'll be your toes next and then your other extremities. You mark my words."

116

The others mumbled agreement.

I tore off the gloves and exposed my tattoos. "Good Heavens," said Old Mrs Pemberton, squinting hard. "It's Hitler."

"No it's not, it's Ian Botham," said Mrs Hargreaves. "And who's that on the other hand? Is it the Archbishop of Canterbury? Or is it Marilyn Monroe? It's hard to tell with all those purple veins."

"They're shadows," I shouted. "Toning."

"Well, who are they?" demanded Mrs Hargreaves. "And I better warn you, they won't come off. Wait a minute, I know who it is, it's Mrs Thatcher and isn't that that monkey that climbs the Empire State building?"

I blame Gerald. He told me he could do a good likeness of Fred Astaire and Ginger Rogers.

THURS FEB 28TH

Natalie is standing for the council. This was the startling news that greeted me when I arrived at Marge's this morning to effect my weekly change of underwear.

"I'm standing as a Moderate Marxist," she informed me.

"Are they different from ordinary Marxists?" I enquired. "Don't they chain themselves to American missile bases like the rest of the Trots?"

"We're a serious alternative to the Labour Left or the Red Wets as we call them."

"Is Harold Wilson going to help you with your campaign?"

"I'm no longer going out with Harold," returned Natalie icily. "Harold is now shacking up with a rival candidate."

"Not a Conservative?"

"No, Walter, not a Conservative. Hortense Venables is a five foot nothing Gambian social worker who is standing as an independent. Her main platform seems to be the abolition of animals fouling the streets."

"Dwarf Black Wimmin Against Natural Refuse, eh? Should be some votes in that I suppose. You Marxists have some competition there. Most people are not keen on walking in unlimited piles of dog dirt."

"A problem doubtless exacerbated in Hortense's case by her height or rather lack of it," smiled Natalie sweetly. "In some streets she must be up to her neck in it."

Neville peered from behind the pages of the Financial Times. "With your views on supporting the minority underdog, I'm surprised you don't vote Tory in this borough. There's so few of us left we're having to disband the cricket team. At this rate by next year we'll be lucky to make up a four at bridge."

"Come on now, Neville, the Conservative Club is the bastion of local commerce and trade in this town."

"The centre of vice and intrigue more like," said Marge who had not forgotten the unfortunate incident of Neville's true-blue mistress.

"I think I might stand for this election," I said. "Is it too late?"

"Whatever would you have to campaign about?" asked Marge. "At eighty-four, you can't have much left worth fighting for unless it's extra Scott's Emulsion in the cold spells as defined by Mrs Thatcher."

"Well, for a start, I think the government ought to provide satisfaction for those senior citizens who have their partner cruelly taken away from them due to the fullness of time."

"You mean, issue hot water bottles? Anyway, your partner was not cruelly taken from you. She left of her own accord with a Yugoslavian grid cleaner twenty years her junior."

"I mean satisfaction. At my age I shouldn't have to compete on the open market for women to lavish my pent-up lust on. They should be provided by the State along with the Christmas bonus and Damart underwear in the winter."

"You don't mean prostitutes?" exclaimed Marge, so shocked she burnt a hole in her puce leg-warmers with the steam iron.

"They don't have to be prostitutes. They can be secretaries or stockbrokers so long as they provide the service."

"How disgusting," said Marge.

"But it's medical," I insisted. "It's sexual therapy, it's a health service, what we pay our stamps for. The women don't have to enjoy it."

"Having relations with men of eighty-four can hardly be construed as enjoyment, Walter."

"Unless you're eighty-four yourself, I suppose," interspersed Neville thoughtfully.

Natalie flared. "Has it never occurred to you that old ladies might prefer the attentions of younger men anyway? They're probably all too grateful that crumblies like yourself are not pestering them. I think there should be places where old ladies can be serviced, as you so offensively put it, by government trained young men called up as a form of National Service."

"Natalie!" exclaimed Marge in horror. "I don't know where your father and I went wrong. We always brought you up to be clean living. Put you in the Enid Blyton Fan Club, let you listen to Donny Osmond records and papered your bedroom with posters of Mr Heath."

Neville joined in. "I always said we were wrong to let her go to Brownies. That Pink Owl was a blatant Marxist if ever I saw one. The Elf Pack was just a training group for the Red Army."

"I might put up for the council myself," I said.

"You? At your age? What would you stand for? No, let me guess, the National Front. A better future for the Over Nineties."

"I'd stand for the Liberals."

"Why the Liberals?"

"Well I wouldn't mind spending a few hours with that Mrs Pomfret the Liberal chairman."

"Chairperson, Walter," corrected Natalie.

"I must say, that's a poor reason for putting up for election, having an uncontrollable desire for the Liberal leader."

"Oh, Mr Thorpe's still in then, is he?" said Marge. "I thought he'd retired to his photography business."

"Maybe you could get the sympathy vote, Walter. They could push you around on a cart in your old clothes with a sign saying 'Look what happens to you when you vote Conservative'."

"The Conservatives aren't in power on this council otherwise we'd all be a lot better off," said Neville. "And God knows what would happen if you got in with your Moderate Marxists! We'd probably have to pay a street tax to walk down to the Post Office, and still get our shoes covered in dog dirt."

"I'm voting for this friend of Natalie's," said Marge. "I've always been against dog dirt, except in the proper place."

"There isn't a proper place for it, that's the point," said Neville. "If the Conservatives got in, we'll provide toilets for them like they do in France. Pissoirs."

Now I've heard it all. I went down to the Over 60's for the free Bingo. Jim Evans was there surrounded by a group of people.

"I'm thinking of standing for the council, Walter," he said. "Independent, of course. Pensioners against Nuclear Attack by Arabs."

"Sorry, Jim," I said. "You're too late for my vote. I'm throwing my lot in with Screaming Lord Sutch."

FRI MARCH 1ST

Amazing news. Ron Alley and Mrs Newfoundland are getting married tomorrow. It was Ron's birthday today and he was expecting the usual sort of present from his loved one, new blades for his corn remover outfit, a gift-wrapped tin of Complan or a gift voucher from the Golden Age Funeral Parlour (motto—'save for your grave').

"I've got something very exciting for you, Ronald," Mrs Newfoundland beamed as I joined them in their apartment for morning tea and hardened Victoria sponge cake. She's taken to calling him Ronald to try and install a presidential aura. "Would you like to guess what it is?"

"It's not a tortoise, is it?"

"Why would I buy you a tortoise?" she asked, puzzled. "We live in a first floor flat with only a window box instead of a garden. Even at a tortoise's rate of knots, it wouldn't take it long to topple over to eternity when you put it out to do something."

"I suppose so," agreed Ron mournfully.

"And, furthermore, it might hit somebody on the head and then you'd be sued for unlimited damages for striking an unknown person with a flying reptile."

"I didn't know tortoises *did* anything," I remarked. They looked at me strangely. "I mean, you never see big lumps of anything around them, do you, like cows and horses. But they do eat don't they so I suppose there must be something somewhere."

"Well whatever it is, it'll stain and smell and I wouldn't want it on my lounge carpet," declared Mrs Newfoundland.

Ron Alley shook his head. "So it's not a tortoise, then? I'm glad really. You can't talk to them like dogs or cats because they can't nod their heads, you know. They just poke them out like those little weathermen ornaments."

"It's more exciting than a tortoise." Mrs Newfoundland tried again to inject a sense of anticipation and celebration into the proceedings.

"It's not a pair of those crotchless knee length thermal underpants I saw is it, for men with poor circulation and high expectations?"

"Just the sort of suggestion we'd expect from *you*, Mr Sherlock." She turned to Ron Alley and tickled him nauseatingly under the chin. "It's something he'll love. I've got us a special licence to wed. We're booked in at the Town Hall at eleven tomorrow."

"Do you want a best man?" I asked quickly although, in view of Ron's previous predilections, I wondered if a best woman might be more appropriate.

"You can be a witness, Mr Sherlock, if you wish. And I would be grateful if you could arrange an evening's entertainment for Ron's stag night, nothing too exciting you'll understand. We don't want his heart giving out before the ring's on his finger."

"Perhaps a visit to the madrigal concert at the Denis Compton Road United Reform Church followed by a late night cocoa at the Salvation Army Home," I suggested, but Ron wanted something more adventurous.

"We'll get a few of the lads down to the Over 60's and maybe book a couple of turns," he said later as we stood with Jim Evans and Albert Gouldman in the queue for our new bus passes. Albert offered to come out of retirement for the evening and perform his magic act but most of us remembered his last performance and declined the offer. Old Mrs Pemberton's finger has healed but is now permanently bent as a result of Albert's guillotine trick and she has terrible trouble doing up her liberty bodice.

"I know a good Punch and Judy show," said Jacob Dickins who had joined us in the queue.

"This is a stag night not a bloody puppet theatre."

"Yes, I know. In the stag show, Mr Punch's biggest protuberance isn't his nose if you catch my meaning."

"Do you mean his wedding tackle?" asked Jim Evans naively.

Jacob nodded. "Modelled on the Eiffel Tower. And the show ends where he obliges Judy on the kitchen floor."

Jim Evans shook his head. "I think we'll settle for the madrigals and cocoa, like Walter says. No sense in scaring him the night before his honeymoon."

"No, no," I said. "You haven't seen Mrs Newfoundland. She's a maneater. A month in Amsterdam would be no preparation for a night with that woman."

"I don't think the funds would stretch to Amsterdam," said Jim Evans.

"And I can't go in a plane with my pacemaker," said Albert, "or my heart'll blow up."

We settled for an evening's bingo at the Holy Mother of Mary. The trouble with the Over 60's is they've got no go about them. I'm thinking of booking one of those 18-30 holidays in Greece. They should be a bit livelier.

SAT MARCH 2ND

Ron Alley and Mrs Newfoundland were duly married at the Town Hall in a simple ceremony attended by myself and Jim Evans as witnesses, Tom Murray, the landlord, and Albert Gouldman who kept a parrot on his shoulder throughout the ceremony.

"It's an advert for my new act," he explained. "All publicity is good publicity and I figured there would be a few cameras about today."

"What's the new act?" I enquired.

His face contorted. "Ya—ya—ya ya."

"Christ, he's having a stroke!" I cried. I tried to remember my first aid training so, taking him by the lapels, I shook him vigorously. "Say something Albert," I shouted.

He rearranged his face. "Ventriloquism," he said, normally. "I can throw my voice without moving my lips, look! Ya—ya—ya—ya."

"Steady on," I said. "You'll frighten the parrot and it'll fly off."

"Very unlikely, Walter," he said. "It was stuffed a week last Thursday."

When the nuptial bonds had been tied and I'd lent Ron Alley the money for the Registrar, we all went across to the Lew Grade Tearooms to celebrate with white sandwiches and Mantunna tea.

"That's a sign of class," said the new Mrs Alley, nodding across to Ron, "a man who puts *French* mustard on his Spam."

"I hope you'll both be very happy," said Tom Murray, "and I'd like to commemorate your change of status from passing guest to joint tenant by raising your rent by £2 a week, to account for the extra wear on my carpets."

"A man of compassion that," I said. "He could easily have put it up a fiver."

At one o'clock Ron and Mrs Alley left us. "We're getting back to the flat now," she said, "to start the honeymoon early."

Some people have all the luck. I had to spend my Saturday afternoon watching Queens Park Rangers.

SUN MARCH 3RD

I've joined an amateur group of entertainers called 'The Last Legs', so named, I would think, because most of its members are on them. They tour the old people's homes and hospitals, giving their services free, forcing their minimal talents onto people too frail or ill to move out of the way.

Jacob Dickins, it was, who persuaded me to go along. He had been thrown out of the North End Players for acting out of turn in 'The Constant Wife'. Originally cast as the butler, he came out after the interval, took the wrong position onstage and started to speak the husband's lines. Everything was thrown into turmoil. The real husband tried to pretend he was the butler but the wife became so confused that she started to speak the lines attributed to Lady Bracknell in 'The Importance of Being Earnest', a part she had held in a previous production. At this point the curtain was brought down and the audience were refunded 50p of their entrance fee, the other 50p being confiscated for their instant coffee and rich tea biscuits.

"I'm better off without it," he said. "They were a load of wankers were the North End Players. I'd been in them eighteen years and only ever played a butler. They just couldn't recognise real talent."

"Are 'The Last Legs' any better?" I asked.

"Shouldn't think so. But the women are better looking. There's one there I've got my eye on who's the spitting image of Clara Bow."

"You mean, if she had lived?" I enquired icily. "Not many nonagenarians I know that you'd describe as 'good lookers'."

The organiser of the group certainly didn't come into that category. She was six foot tall with an enlarged Adams Apple and a grey pencil moustache, not unlike an ageing David Niven.

"She does the recruiting," one old lady told me. "I saw her coming but I couldn't get my zimmer out of the way quick enough and next thing I knew she'd made me into a member. I have to sing George Formby's 'Leaning on a Lamp Post' without my bottom teeth as one half of a cabaret duo. The other half, Mrs Gibbon, plays the banjo, but due to her advanced arthritis she can only pluck the string nearest her which restricts our range somewhat."

"She's called Maud Ackers, the woman that runs it," said Mrs Gibbon. "And she seems to work on the opposite principle to 'horses for courses'. Like making that man in the grey scarf play the trumpet when he's got emphysema. I mean, he'll never get anywhere as good as Eddie Calvert, will he? Not when he's calling for an oxygen mask every time he blows top C and he's ninety if he's a day."

"Hardly worthwhile getting his publicity shots developed," I murmured.

Maud Ackers approached me. "You look a nimble little chappie," she said. "You can be part of my sand dancing troupe. We're going to do an updated version of Wilson, Kepple and Betty. Which do you want to be?"

"Not Betty, if you don't mind," I said. "I've got an aversion to French knickers against the skin. Could I take Wilson?"

"Certainly," she boomed. "In which case, you can be Kepple." She turned to Jacob Dickins. "And I'll be Betty myself, so that's settled." She strode away, notebook in hand.

Jacob looked worried. "I didn't like to mention it, Walter, you know, about having just one leg. Somehow, it never got a chance to creep casually into the conversation. It could prove an obstacle in a dancing role."

"I shouldn't worry, Jacob," I reassured him. "That bloke Kepple was probably working well within his limits with two. I'd just go along and take a chance. Funny thing to have, a sand dancing act."

123

"Well you know why, don't you?" said Jacob. "Her cat died the other day so she wanted to find a new use for the litter tray."

Old Mrs Pemberton was chosen to play Betty Grable in a sketch about the War Years. "It was a case of stamina," she wheezed. "The other ladies had shaplier legs but I had the strongest elastic in my surgical stockings."

Our meeting was held in the temporary Anderson Air Raid Shelter in Kaiser Avenue which also houses the headquarters of the Mobile Library Service, a group of council employees who travel deprived housing estates in a reinforced riot van distributing illicit copies of Little Black Sambo to National Front children in contradiction of the Gay Left Council's instructions.

"There aren't many young members are there?" I whispered to Jacob. After Mrs Newfoundland, I don't think I could respond to the ministrations of an older woman, especially one who might have first hand memory of Princess Mary of Teck as a young girl. In fact, it would take a posse of scantily clad nubile beauty queens to rival the attraction of a mug of Benger's Food in my bedroom.

"There's a retired striptease dancer in the cast," said Jacob. "Calls herself Lolita but she had her Golden Wedding before Prince William was born. She used to be part of those tableaux where the unclothed woman never had to move a muscle."

"She'll be all right here, then," I remarked. "She needn't rise from her wheelchair."

Jacob became excited. "Onstage, she wears a black and yellow basque made out of rubber with her white skin squeezing out from all sides. Looks like a giant wasp stuck in a toothpaste tube. Drives the old men in the nursing homes wild. Three of them had to have injections to put them to sleep in case their hearts gave out."

"They'd be better giving her the injection and save us all the spectacle."

Maud Ackers returned with a large tray of cat litter. "Let's see you perform in that," she said.

"I think I'll stick to the Gents if it's all the same to you," I said but Jacob had already stepped in and was hopping about like Long John Silver.

"You'd think she'd have cleaned it after the cat," I said, "but I suppose that encourages you to be nimble."

Maud Ackers stooped and picked out a brown object. "It was only a leaf, Wilson," she said. "Now jump in and we'll do it together." She pulled me onto the tray and we jumped about on the cat litter like St Vitus. "Come on, Kepple, use your other leg."

Jacob lowered his wooden appendage but it skidded on the tray and he pulled us all down into the litter.

I spent most of the night tossing and turning in bed trying to get bits of grit out of my combinations. I am giving up the stage. Maybe I shall join a fencing club, a lot less energetic.

MON MARCH 4TH

This afternoon, I attended an emergency meeting of the Social Security Anniversary Club. This is a friendly gathering of idle loafers and scroungers who, to be eligible for membership, have to have been living off the State for at least twelve months. In fact, some members can boast of over twenty years of uninterrupted sponging.

Having enjoyed only seven weeks of government handouts, I was not strictly eligible but Jim Evans persuaded me to go along. "Slip a bluey to the Treasurer," he advised, "and you'll be in for life. Think of the social benefits to joining a club like this. In the past twelve months, we've been to Gadaffi Street Gasworks, the Holy Mother of Mary Giant Chrysanthemum Show, a tour of the town's sewage works and at Christmas we all get a parcel containing a black pudding, a Kiwi fruit and a bottle of Carter's Little Liver Pills."

The emergency meeting was called to discuss the changes in Housing Benefits proposed by the Government.

"I can't afford to pay out of my own pocket," moaned a fat mother of three. "Not and have our annual holiday in Bermuda. And, while they're at it, what about free uniforms for the children?"

"Are they in the SS?" I enquired.

"They're at the Gregory Peck Comprehensive," she retorted, "though I suppose there isn't that much difference."

I had never realised there were all these things the Government provided free of charge. And to think, only last week, I signed an agreement to rent a budgie for 25p a week as an insurance against loneliness and morbid tendencies.

If the budgie should die in the next five years, I am guaranteed a replacement bird of similar hue and disposition. The seed is extra.

"The thing to do is sublet," said Mrs Sandford. "I get £25 a week towards my rent but I have four miners who stay with me weekends and they bring in £50."

"And we all know what benefits they get for their money," sniggered Jim Evans. "I've seen them queueing up outside her door with their Humphrey Davy lamps stuck on their heads like eagles' beaks and lascivious

125

expressions on their dirty faces like a row of manic Al Jolsons. I wouldn't mind but she was old when Budge Patty won Wimbledon."

"Budge Patty?" said Jim Evans. "Isn't he that fellow that's living with Mrs Wicklow in Vertigo Street who used to keep ferrets in her outdoor lavatory?"

"You've got to be careful about that co-habiting," warned a brown-eyed man with unnaturally large ears and an Arthur Scargill hairpiece. "They spy on you from unmarked cars, to see if you go into the same bedroom."

"What happens if you do?" asked Jim Evans curiously.

He looked blank. "I dunno. I suppose they force their way in, hoping to catch you at it, and throw a bucket of water over you and warn you not to do it again according to the 1984 Rent Act."

"They can be very painful, ferrets," I said. "Arthur Meadowcroft used to keep two down his trousers."

"Don't be ridiculous," said Mrs Sandford. "Why would he keep two ferrets down his trousers?"

"I don't know," I said. "Company for each other I suppose."

"You'll be coming to the Seminar next week," asked Jim Evans, "on Moonlighting? All the members here are very keen on Moonlighting. It's their contribution to Mrs Thatcher's vision of private enterprise. Without Moonlighting, God knows how some of us would have been able to buy our British Gas shares."

I'm glad I've joined this club. It seems to be more go-ahead than Neville's Conservative Club but run along similar lines.

TUES MARCH 5TH

Called at Marge and Neville's on the way home from the Afternoon Tea Dance. It was Marge's birthday and they were celebrating with a Victoria sponge and packet jelly. Halfway through the bloater paste sandwiches, I had a funny turn and slumped to the table.

Marge rushed round the table to undo my collar. "I think he's dead," she cried. "And we never did find out the number of the safe deposit box."

"I'm here," I croaked weakly. "I'm still with you."

Neville ran to the phone. "I'm getting an ambulance," he said.

"Bugger the ambulance," cried Marge. "Get the number of his box."

"It's my face," I whined. "I can't feel my face. My mouth's numb. I think I've had a stroke."

"Did you hit it on the table when you fell?"

"He couldn't have done," said Neville, "his fall was broken by the wild cherry blancmange. Look, his face is covered in it." He ambled to the telephone.

"Lucky he didn't drown," commented Marge. "I suppose it must be a stroke then. You'd have thought he'd have waited till he finished his sandwiches. That was best butter I put on those."

"Ambulance," Neville said into the phone in a matter of fact voice normally reserved for ordering a takeaway pizza. He gave the address, there was a pause, then, "He's eighty-four."

"Don't tell them that," I cried. "They'll think it's not worth their while coming."

"Just lie still in that blancmange," soothed Marge. "Help is coming. I don't think he's got long," she whispered loudly to Neville. "You'll be as right as rain in a minute," she said to me.

"Can you move your toes?" Neville shouted in my ear.

"I can't see if I can or not," I said. "I've got my shoes on."

"Perhaps he's drunk. I knew I put too much sherry in that trifle. The fumes must have got to him."

"Fetch me a naked woman," I cried. "If I'm going to die, I want to die happy."

"We'll have no naked women in this house," said Marge. "I'm not having Neville excited again so soon after Christmas."

"I'll get some smelling salts," said Neville.

"What do you want those for? He's awake isn't he? Just let him mumble on. It's obvious he's delirious."

"I've just thought," said Marge suddenly. "Did he come for his clean combinations last Thursday only we can't have him going to the Hospital in those awful things he's had on since February. And you'd better go through his pockets and make sure there's nothing in them that might upset the doctor at the Post Mortem."

"Hang on," I said. "I might recover."

The ambulance arrived before they could search me and I was taken off to the Otis Redding Memorial Hospital where I lie now, under the observation of a team of hopeful medical students. Apparently, I am to be a question in their examination. Things are not looking good.

WED MARCH 6TH

Spent the day in the Otis Redding Memorial Hospital having tests to ascertain the cause of my unfortunate collapse into Marge's wild cherry blancmange.

I was divested of my hospital issue pyjamas and my combinations and put into a thin white sheet which the nurse told me could be used as a winding sheet in the event of my unexpected demise as they were trying to cut down on the laundry bills.

I was then placed into a pre-war wheelchair and transported to a busy public corridor where the porter bade me good day and left me. The door at the end of the corridor led onto the street and a fierce March gale blew through it, not only making me bitterly cold but also blowing the winding sheet above my knees and exposing my personal regions to passing strangers.

Luckily, we were en route to the Ophthalmic Department so most of the passing strangers were half blind and unable to notice anything unusual, not that there is, of course, anything unusual to be seen down there.

The minutes passed by and nobody approached me. My face was now more numb than the previous day but I attributed this to frostbite. Eventually, I fell asleep and woke to find myself being wheeled outside to a Portacabin at the back of the main building. I could not see who was pushing me but it turned out to be a man because I heard him call out, "Another one for the shed, Harry, I don't know what they're putting in them dinners but they've been dropping like flies this week."

"It's not the dinners, it's the new surgeon they've got in the Heart Shop. I think he must have been on a free transfer from the Punjab Infirmary. His hands shake so much he can hardly hold his chopsticks at breakfast. Denis from Premature Senility put a xylophone by his corn flakes one morning and he was playing it for ten minutes with his chopsticks before he could get his wrists under control. Not what you want when you're swapping hearts about."

"Well it's the veins isn't it. Mix *them* up and you've got Spaghetti Junction in your patient's insides and they're no fun to unravel aren't veins."

"Not with shaking hands at any rate. And if you get a knot, you daren't cut it out and start again, not with a vein. They start to bleed you know and then you're in trouble."

I sat up. "Excuse me," I said, "but I've decided to discharge myself. I only came in with minor faceache and it's suddenly miraculously better."

The effect of my little speech was startling. My driver emitted a loud scream and dropped to the ground in a dead faint. The man called Harry crossed himself and stared open-mouthed as I rose unsteadily from the chair. Then in a dramatic gesture, he ripped a cheap imitation silver crucifix from his neck and held it aloft between us crying out unintelligibly in a foreign tongue.

"Kindly direct me to the observation ward," I said, "where I may pick up my clothes." He said nothing but pointed back to the main building. Pulling the winding sheet around me I set off. I had reached Casualty when a man in a white coat stopped me. "We've been looking all over for you," he said. "And what have you done with our wheelchair?" His eyes narrowed. "Haven't sold it, have you?"

I explained that I had been on my way to the incinerator when, by extreme good fortune, I had woken up. Otherwise I would now be partly dissected in the Post Mortem Lab or already burnt and helping fuel the hospital central heating system.

"Don't think I don't know what those big chimneys are for," I told him. "Your average patient may delude himself they are for the hospital kitchens but I've seen pictures of Dachau on television. I know."

"Mr Sherlock, attractive though the idea of putting you in the hospital ovens may be, all we really want is a sample of your blood for testing."

"Are you suggesting I've got Aids?"

"I think it highly unlikely that you have been in a position to catch Aids in the last twenty years."

"You don't kid me with that innocent stuff. I know you can catch it at the Baths. I never go swimming in the public baths without one of those condoms on."

"I always prefer swimming trunks myself. I find them more sartorially elegant than a plain condom. Or do you wear Designer Condoms?" He started to walk on. "Anyway, I haven't got all day so follow me. All I want is a little prick."

"Most people I know wish the opposite," I said. "I suppose it's with you being Chinese, is it? Chinese women are different to us aren't they? Is it true you have to face the North Pole during congress or is that the Arabs?"

"I believe you are referring to the Muslims and it is the East."

"Ah yes," I said. "Towards Bradford, very appropriate."

We reached the Pathology Lab. "If you'll wait here," he said "Someone will come and see to you in a moment."

I watched him disappear and settled down for another long wait. After ten minutes, I got cramp in my left leg and had to stand on my right one at which point a nurse appeared. "Looking for Maternity?" she asked breezily.

"No," I replied. "Do I look pregnant?"

She pointed to my leg. "I thought you were the stork."

"Very funny," I said. "I've been waiting here so long, I wouldn't be at all surprised if gangrene hasn't set in."

"I hope not," she said. "We only do amputations on a Tuesday and today's Wednesday so you'll have a long wait. Now, are you going to let me have some blood instead?"

"I can't spare much," I said. "I've got pernicious anaemia." She ignored me and led me into the laboratory where she stuck a needle into my arm and drew off a teaspoonful of blood.

"I see what you mean," she said, looking at it closely. "It's very pale and thin. I wouldn't want to eat a black pudding made out of this."

"I'd be obliged if you'd stop referring to me as offal," I objected. "And if you've finished with me, I want to get dressed before I catch double pneumonia."

"There's X-Ray yet," she said. "Bottom of the corridor, first left, second right, third left past the boiler house."

"I don't need an X-Ray," I said.

"Just to see if you broke anything when you fell."

"The only thing I could have broken is the blancmange bowl," I said. "Do you want to X-Ray that? I'm certainly not going under one of those machines. They make you sterile."

"Would that matter too much," she enquired, "at your age?"

"I'm hoping to start a large family," I said, "if I ever get out of here."

I was taken back to the ward and put into more ill-fitting pyjamas. "Just missed tea," smiled the ward sister, "but never mind because Doctor is here to take a specimen."

The doctor was a large ginger-haired Irishman. "Another whitey," I groaned. "Can't this hospital afford brown doctors?"

He held out a test-tube. "I want you to relieve yourself in this, Mr Sherlock."

"From here?" I cried.

He grimaced patiently. "No, you may stand a little closer. We may even let you hold it yourself providing you try not to overfill it. The cleaners don't come until morning."

"Better than the amputators," I pointed out. "They only come on a Wednesday."

I started to fill the test tube and he consulted a clipboard. "When did you last have coitus, Mr Sherlock?"

"Let me see, it must be two months last Tuesday, after an Indian curry."

"Is the curry significant?"

"I think the one led to the other," I said.

"Funny. I've never heard of curry as an aphrodisiac. Might I ask who your partner was, just in case we need to contact her under the Spread of Infectious Diseases Act of 1876?"

"Partner? I didn't have a partner. I was on my own at the time."

"How could you have coitus alone?"

"Quite easily really. I ate the curry, I got the grips and next thing I threw up over Mrs Newfoundland's cat."

The red Mick clenched his teeth. "I think you are referring to colitis, Mr Sherlock. Coitus means sexual relations. Have you had sexual relations in the last eight years?"

"Since Mrs Thatcher came into office, you mean, although I don't suppose there's a connection. In fact, though, I've had sexual relations for forty years. My Auntie Alma was a very sexual person."

"What I mean is," he was almost shouting, "have you enjoyed any lovemaking in the past eight years?"

"Enjoyed it?" I asked. "No, I can honestly say I've enjoyed none of it. My partners have not been very enthusiastic about it, you see, and I found it dampened my ardour. So, no, suffered it would be more to the point."

"Would you be able to trace your partners if necessary?"

"If you've got a copy of Who's Who," I said, "I'd be able to take you to them tomorrow."

At this point he left, taking his half filled test tube with him.

Remembering my previous stay at the Otis Redding Memorial Hospital and my difficulty in sleeping due to the noisy emissions of the bowel patients, I managed to procure earplugs for the night.

No word yet from Marge. She is probably sulking because she had to make a replacement wild cherry blancmange.

THURS MARCH 7TH

Three days before my 85th birthday, and Neville and Marge have had me put away. I am now a permanent resident of the John Lennon Memorial Home for Infirm Gentlefolk.

Neville has had to pay £350 for a private operation to remove a condom from my personal regions, courtesy of BUPA—something any son would do for his old father.

I had to go private as Neville could not bear the humilitation of my complaint being discussed at the Otis Redding Memorial Hospital where Marge's Aunt works as a Relief Slops Collector on alternate Saturdays.

She would have been likely to spill the beans at the Conservative Club.

My doctor was called Mohammed and I thought I'd struck lucky and managed to get an Indian one at last instead of the white ones they give you on the National Health, but she turned out to be a Bernadette Mohammed, an Irish nurse who'd made good.

She seemed bemused that I'd used the Superglue in the first place until I explained that the condom had kept slipping off on the previous evening when I failed to sustain my excitement during the Ladies Excuse-me Barn Dance Classes at the Over 60's.

Marge thought it disgusting that I should wear a condom at all until I pointed out to her, if you get one thick enough, it helps keep you warm in winter thus obviating the need for those horsehair combinations with thermal properties that make your calves itch.

My reasons for needing the condom in the first place were in case Mrs Winkle succumbed to my advances on the 9.47 bus home from the Baptist Chapel where they give lectures to pensioners on The Final Journey. None of us are keen to embark on the Final Journey (Mrs Winkle thinks it is the 10.38 bus) and only two are Baptists in a crowd of non-believers and active Pagans, but they give free tea and lobster paste sandwiches.

Had Mrs Winkle invited me in for weak tea and individual custard tart, my problem would have been how to innocently introduce the condom. As she is 72, I could hardly say I didn't want to get her pregnant. However, producing the condom out of the blue would be tantamount to suggesting she might have Aids, 24 years after her late husband's demise from an unexplained skin complaint in the Lancashire Fusiliers.

However, IF I WAS ALREADY WEARING THE CONDOM, it might not be noticed in the general maelstrom of asthmatic passion.

In the event, it was not to be. I missed the bus and Mrs Winkle was converted to Buddhism during her journey by an Irish vest salesman with boils from Kilburn.

I, meanwhile, ended up at Marge and Neville's in some discomfort from the Superglue. Marge wanted to use a chisel but Neville opted for the operation provided I went into a home for my own safety.

I may take up Celibacy and put up for Pope.

FRI MARCH 8TH

My first full day in the John Lennon Memorial Home for Infirm Gentlefolk. I was taken round to meet the other residents, many of whom were in comatose conditions able hardly to raise a bony finger in greeting.

In the hall is a Suggestion Box into which we are invited to contribute our ideas to make the home "a happier and more exciting place to live in".

This idea of "Inmate participation" is not a philosophy I subscribe to. Institutions like Nursing Homes, Prisons and Television Companies need the strong rule of benevolent dictatorship. We need look no further than our beloved leader, Mrs Thatcher, to support this doctrine. Here is a woman who gets things done without the interference of lackeys and in happy ignorance of so-called advice from her "supporters".

With the aid of a plastic knife from the dining room, I was able to extract some of the suggestions from the box to find out which issues of the day the residents were campaigning on. They were not world-shattering. A Mrs Harris wanted to treble the lunchtime helpings of custard, there were two requests for the official issue of thermal bedsocks to be extended until February, and a Mrs Welsby wanted gears fitted to her zimmer to assist her on the steep incline approaching the Emergency Lavatory on the ground floor.

All in all, not a revolutionary collection. After much deliberation, I posted my own suggestion although I am not hopeful it will be implemented.

SAT MARCH 9TH

My contribution to the Suggestion Box was not well received. The Bursar, Mr Vickerstaffe, read it out at Assembly which takes place in the Great Hall after breakfast.

The main purpose of Assembly is not religious. Rather it is a means of sorting out those able to crawl from their beds from the unfortunates who have expired during the night. A time and motion study declared it saved the nurses time walking the corridors checking the bedrooms for corpses.

"Mr Sherlock has proposed the installation of a contraceptive machine in the gents' toilet." Mr Vickerstaffe's eyes rolled about like a pinball machine as a gasp of horror ran through the company. "An unnecessary request, I would have thought, in view of the fact that the average age of the lady inmates of this establishment is 74½."

Weak ribald laughter greeted this comment and I jumped to my feet in protest. "Who said anything about these old bats? I was thinking more of the staff."

"Do you imagine my nurses are going to be physically attracted to a toothless 84-year-old man with no hair and rubber sheets?"

What *is* this thing about false teeth? Two thirds of the nation's over-35's have them and they are certainly an improvement on the black rotting stumps our ancestors wore.

SUN MARCH 10TH

My 85th birthday. I got new woollen combinations and a tin of diabetic grape juice from Marge and Neville, delivered by messenger as the note inside said they were too busy to attend due to a re-run of 'Gardeners' Question Time' on Radio 4.

However, Jim Evans called in with a mid-year diary—July to June. At my great age, he said, he couldn't risk waiting until January for the normal one.

Natalie also came bearing a cake with a candle in the middle. "Sorry it's a bit sticky, Walter," she said, "only I'd no icing sugar so I slapped some frozen blancmange on top instead." It looked suspiciously like Marge's Wild Cherry.

Matron gave a small party in the dining room at teatime, which those residents still able to stand attended. They all sang Happy Birthday as I blew out the candle and we ate mince pies left over from Christmas. My suggestion for a game of Postman's Knock with the night nurses was ignored, but Nurse Kitchen, who is brown with dyed ash blonde hair, winked at me in a lascivious manner which inspired a belief in better things to come.

MON MARCH 11TH

The Wrath of Matron descended on me over breakfast. Apparently, due to cataracts, she'd failed to notice that the candle on my birthday cake from Natalie was a giant wax effigy of the Bishop of Durham, or rather an enlarged selection portion of His Holiness, as sold by Sextoys of Millom.

However, a Polaroid photo of the iced confection, taken before the conflagration, had been shown to the Governors. Despite being nuns, they were not amused.

Stewart Dangerfield in the next bed (93, chronic cirrhosis, enuresis and halitosis) said they were only upset because it melted before they could impale themselves on it.

Matron was not amused and ordered double injections for him. He should sleep till April.

TUES MARCH 12TH

An ambulance arrived first thing to take Mrs Harris to hospital. The word in the dining room was that she'd taken an overdose of Complan, the only known method of self-destruction available at the John Lennon Memorial Home since the silver service was replaced by plastic knives.

I retreated to my bed after breakfast, feigning sickness, in the hope Nurse Kitchen would give me a bed bath—but she was too busy with the real thing. Mrs Welsby had been confined to her commode for two days. Now they were thinking of putting castors on it to enable her to be wheeled to the TV lounge to watch 'Dallas' while continuing in her ablutions. Mrs Welsby is the only lady in the Home who receives a sponsored registration from Andrex.

WED MARCH 13TH

Brochures came today from the Blessed Sacrament of the Virgin Mary advertising places in their new graveyard extension. They looked so inviting in full colour pictures that you were almost tempted to do yourself into secure one.

Meantime, a rumour was going around that the JLMH might be up for sale. Arabs are reputed to have offered £450,000 for the property and tangible assets. I suppose the tangible assets means us. I don't know that I want to be owned by Arabs. Look what happened to Shergar. As for Nurse Kitchen, I suppose she'll end up in White Slavery. I might vote for that Mr Kinnock next time in the hope he will nationalize us and save us from foreign hands.

THURS MARCH 14TH

The Easter Outing. Two mini-buses came to take us to the Tower of London. Luckily I was able to escape on arrival and got a No. 15 bus to Soho. Being thirsty, I went into one of the topless bars for a soft drink and was horrified to find myself face to face with a half-naked Nurse Kitchen.

"We Guardian Angels of the Medical Profession have to supplement our incomes somehow, Mr Sherlock," she explained, taking my £5 in exchange for a minute orange juice. "It's what our dear Prime Minister calls private enterprise." She leaned across the counter, her full bosom dangling against my war medals. "If you like, I'll have a dance with you later and bring over a bottle of imitation champagne. It'll only cost you £30."

"Do you do extra services?" I asked excitedly

135

"Only cutting your toenails when I'm on duty again this evening."

It wasn't what I had in mind. The sooner Mrs Thatcher opens state-run brothels with Pensioners' Passes the better.

FRI MARCH 15TH

Amazing news. The Arabs *have* bought the JLMH but they are turning it into a Holiday Home for Unemployed Miners. We are all to be evicted immediately to enable building work to start on the jacuzzis, indoor swimming pools, cinema complex, and all the necessities that unemployed miners need to maintain their quality of life.

Marge and Neville arrived after lunch to reluctantly take me home. "I want no more funny business when you come back," said Marge. "You'll eat my roast beef and Spotted Dick and like it. And no going out after 9 p.m. or having your disgusting friends round with Methodist leanings. You've got to start acting your age. It's time you took up the Bible and long afternoon naps."

"What about my exercise?"

"You can do the Daily Telegraph Crossword. That should keep you active."

So much for "Life Begins at 80."

I've decided to leave home . . .